Witch at Odds

A Jinx Hamilton Mystery

Book Two

Juliette Harper

Skye House Publishing, LLC
4517 Ranch View Road
Fort Worth, TX 76109

Edited by Patricia Pauletti
Cover design by SkyeBookDesigns.com

Print ISBN: 978-1-943516-87-2

First Edition: January 2016

Witch at Odds

A JINX HAMILTON
MYSTERY

Book Two

DEDICATION

Prettier the flower, the farther from the path.

Stephen Sondheim, *Into the Woods*

ACKNOWLEDGMENTS

As always, we would like to thank our readers. You are such an important part of the magic. Special thanks to our beta readers, Brenda Trimble, Larry Trimble, and to our faithful and patient proofreader, Sandra Jackson. To Delia Ruth Williamson for the fairy dust. And to Jennifer Radcliff, for her paging and design work, and for being our first and constant friend and mentor in the self-publishing world.

ONE

"What could go wrong?"

Let's just begin with those famous "last" words, shall we?

This whole thing started when I decided to add a room onto the back of the store I inherited from my Aunt Fiona. Okay, that and a few *simple* renovations to implement a really great idea for a coffee shop / espresso bar.

My first mistake was in forgetting to run the plans by the store itself for her approval.

Yeah, you read that right.

My store is . . . well, actually I don't know what my store is, but her name is Myrtle.

Not to be all anthropomorphic or anything, but she's very much a "person."

In the short time I've been in residence, Myrtle has never been anything but helpful, quietly leading me to things in the hopeless jumble that passes for an inventory on request.

She actually has a pretty good sense of humor, and something of a maternal streak. Of course when I was being thick-headed about something early in our relationship, Myrtle did whiz an arrow past my nose, but my own mother threw a knife at me once.

(Okay, *fine*, just in case my mother ever reads this, she

claims her hands were wet and the knife slipped. All I
know is that a sharp piece of cutlery landed at my feet. I
quit arguing and did as I was told. Myrtle achieved much
the same reaction from me with her arrow.)

I should have known Myrtle would prefer to have
things done her way, mainly because my deceased Aunt
Fiona warned me about it. Yes, Aunt Fiona still pops in
from time to time. There's no reason death *has* to be a self-
limiting experience. For heaven's sake, think outside the
box (or the casket as the case may be.)

So, long about now, you're probably wondering if I'm
completely nuts. Probably, but I'm also a witch. That was
Aunt Fiona's other bequest to me—magical powers. The
fact that I'm a newly minted witch goes a long way toward
explaining the story I'm about to tell you.

But, first, let's briefly backtrack. Hi, my name is Jinx
Hamilton. My business sits on the Briar Hollow courthouse
square between Chase McGregor's cobbler shop and
Amity Prescott's art gallery.

Chase is on the fast track to becoming my boyfriend,
and Amity is flaky, creative, and anxious for us to do some
joint functions once my coffee shop is up and running.

Then there's Tori, whose official title in my life is BFF.
She's also my brand new business partner, the fulfillment
of a plan we hatched when we were six and set up our first
lemonade stand.

Tori quit her job at Tom's Cafe and will move into the
room out back once it's finished. It was her idea to do both
construction projects at one time, so technically this was
all her fault. (That's my story and I'm sticking to it.)

The paint gave us the first hint we might be in for trouble. Walking in the store's front door amounts to entering
a time warp. Think antique display cabinets, beautifully
worn wood floors, and an old, elegant tin ceiling. The walls
were a sort of indistinct stucco tannish, white *thing*.

Tori thought some color in the coffee area would help give the place a "funky, bohemian vibe." We're hoping to bring in local musicians on the weekends, and maybe even serve beer and wine if my license application goes through. The whole planned decorating scheme felt right, so I was onboard.

Tori drove over to one of the big box hardware places and picked up a variety of paint samples. The palette ran the gamut from aubergine to chartreuse, but no matter what color she put on the wall, Myrtle instantly turned it to aged tan.

It was all I could do not to laugh, which would have infuriated Tori and encouraged Myrtle.

Tori stood there with her dripping fuchsia paintbrush and glared at the store, which meant her head was on a swivel since we don't exactly know where to look when we talk to Myrtle.

"Knock it off, Myrtle," Tori demanded. "Don't you want to *live* a little?"

Since Myrtle instantly blew Tori a raspberry, we'll assume the answer to that one was "no."

As diplomatically as I could manage, since Tori can be a little . . . *firm minded*, I said, "I don't think it's a good idea to annoy the building we're living in. Why don't we go for retro funky bohemian and keep the . . . uh . . . current, tasteful vintage appeal?"

Still brandishing her paintbrush, Tori wheeled on me and said accusingly, "Suck-up."

"I'm good with that," I said earnestly, "totally."

We abandoned the painting plan for the moment, which I hoped Myrtle would see as a show of support, or even out and out obedience, but as I was about to find out, this dispute was far from over.

The next day, Mark's guys started trying to relocate the floor-to-ceiling wooden cases currently occupying the corner between the staircase and the east wall, which was the area destined to be the coffee bar.

Tori was nowhere to be seen. Earlier in the day, she had run a few errands, and then excused herself to continue her research into proper espresso preparation. That was a fairly adult way to say that she was still ticked off about yesterday and was, frankly, pouting.

Now, understand, I would never actually use the word "pout" with her, but as my mother would have so eloquently put it, if Tori's lower lip had been pushed out any further, she would've tripped over it.

I felt vaguely like a kindergarten teacher attempting to forestall a playground riot.

So, as the men started to move the cabinets, I was the only official witness to what happened next, which was a lot of nothing.

After an impressive amount of grunting, groaning, and suppressed swearing, Mark stood back, scratched his head in obvious puzzlement and said, "The dang things won't budge. Looks like we're going to have to take a crowbar to this situation. It's a shame, because we'll probably destroy the cabinets, but I don't know what else to do."

When he used the word "destroy," Myrtle let out a menacing rattle.

"What the heck was that?" Mark asked, looking around with alarm.

"Just air in the pipes," I lied smoothly.

"Maybe we need to get a plumber in here," he said with concern. "The last thing you want is a flood."

"No, no," I said. "We're good. Give us the night to think about the display cases. We'll talk about it tomorrow. Okay?"

As soon as he was gone, I put my hands on my hips and said, "Okay, Myrtle, you and I have to talk about this situation *now*."

Even I have a hard time taking myself seriously when I'm speaking to thin air, which is why these conversations only take place when the store is empty. That and the fact that if anyone witnessed one of my exchanges with Myrtle, I'd be fitted for a snug jacket with really, really long sleeves.

"Myrtle, look," I said, "I'm sorry. I should have talked to you about our plans before the work started. We're not trying to do anything to hurt you."

Then it dawned on me.

Did the renovations cause Myrtle actual *pain*?

"Oh my God, Myrtle," I said, a note of panic coming into my voice. "Are we hurting you?"

To my immense relief, the rack of Briar Hollow souvenir sun visors by the counter bobbled back and forth in the generally recognized sign for "no."

"Ok, good," I said. "We don't want to hurt you, but we really need you to not be all set in your ways. *I* need you to not be set in your ways. Everything changes, Myrtle, including interior decorating schemes."

Myrtle blew out a long, drawn out exhalation of air. She sounded wearily patient.

"Fine, I'll give you that one," I admitted. "We don't really have a decorating scheme. The whole eclectic thing worked for Aunt Fiona. She kept this place going because she was such a character. I'm a whole lot more ordinary than that, which you apparently like, but Tori isn't ordinary at all."

Case in point. Right now, the ends of my BFF's short, spiky, blond hair are a kind of glowing shade of magenta.

"Tori is going to be living with us," I continued. "She is part of the family. She *will* come up with crazy ideas. It's just who she is. Come on, Myrtle. You lived with Aunt Fiona for years. How can you not be used to crazy?"

Out of nowhere a Polaroid picture of my aunt fluttered

down and landed at my feet. I picked up the snapshot and studied it. That was Aunt Fiona alright. Although she was smiling into the camera with her usual impish expression, the rest of her was remarkably plain. My aunt was wearing what my mother derisively referred to as her "winter uniform." A gray sweatshirt, baggy jeans, and running shoes.

"Are you trying to tell me that Tori is a little bit too colorful for you in the actual sense of *color*?" I asked Myrtle.

A small shower of gold stars fluttered down around me, the kind that teachers give children who cut straight lines with their blunt nosed scissors.

"Okay," I said, ignoring Myrtle's obvious condescension, "how about we compromise. I'll get her to tone down the color, if you'll relax and not be worried about us moving a few things around."

Myrtle answered with a little hum that indicated she was thinking about it. I decided to press my slim advantage with more groveling.

"I know I should have asked your opinion, and I will from now on, but will you please let the guys move the display cases in the morning? They're just going right over there," I said, pointing.

A drawer in one of the cases slid open with remarkable defiance, releasing a paint brush that floated briskly in front of my face and snapped neatly in two. I couldn't help myself; I laughed.

"I get it, I get it," I said. "No painting. But are we good to go on the work to put in the coffee bar? It's just a sink, a work surface, a fridge, and a counter. And there will be some tables right in here." Again, I gestured with my arms.

After a minute, the sun visors nodded.

"Thank you," I said.

I felt like a diplomat who had just avoided a missile launch.

Now for phase two. I had to go upstairs and deal with the other half of the stand off, my BFF who was no doubt sulking on the couch with the cats.

Color me right. That's exactly where I found Tori, but she was *not* in her happy place.

Now, my cats, Zeke, Yule, Xavier and Winston looked like they were having the time of their lives—the comatose time of their lives. All concerned were snoring.

"Hi," I said, claiming the big easy chair. "Myrtle and I had a summit conference. We're good to go on moving the cabinets, but it's thumbs down on the painting still."

"Harrumph," Tori grumbled, scratching Zeke's ears and staring at the TV.

Covering my eyes with my hand and shaking my head, I said, "Seriously, Tori, I think you're outgunned this time. Is going to war with a magical building really the battle you want to pick?"

Tori grabbed one of the sofa pillows and held it defensively against her chest—the same way she used to clutch her teddy bear, Rufus, when we were kids. "I guess not," she admitted glumly. "But my color scheme rocked."

"It did," I said soothingly. "There was rockage. And you can use any color you want in your own room."

"I didn't expect Myrtle to act so freaking *old*," Tori grumbled.

Since this did not seem to be the time to point out that we hadn't expected the store to do anything but sit there and be a building, I opted for Plan B: red wine, popcorn, and repeat binge-watching the last season of *Scandal*.

By three episodes in, Tori was far more interested in debating the merits of Team Jake v. Team Fitz than she was in Myrtle's frame of mind.

(For the record, I have so had enough of Fitz. Dude, just run the country already.)

Sometime around 11, I looked over to see that Tori had joined the feline snooze-fest. I quietly turned off the TV, threw a blanket over her and the cats, and carried my laptop into the bedroom.

Time for class.

Two

No, I wasn't taking a class online, although if I could have found the one I needed, I would have signed up in a heartbeat. You see, Aunt Fiona left me the store and her magic, but neither one came with an owner's manual. But hey, it's the 21st century, so when in doubt, Google!

Yes, I will admit that doesn't have the same metaphysical gravitas as saying that I found her grimoire, a spell book with parchment pages and a dramatic leather cover emblazoned with some occult symbol, but it is the truth.

If I'm going to be completely honest, I was initially so thrown for a loop by the idea that I'm a witch that if I had found a book like that, I probably would've run backwards. Instead, my need for information drove me to much less threatening sources: a search engine, online used bookstores, and eBay.

That night, after settling things with Myrtle about the renovation work, I got back to my other major project—emancipating a cemetery full of ghosts to freely live their afterlives.

After Aunt Fiona showed up post-mortem for the first time, I found out that I can interact with other spirits as well. Technically, I think that makes me a psychic, but the magical semantics are a little too complicated for me to be ordering business cards just yet.

Anyway, the short version of that long story is that I now visit the local cemetery one or two nights a week to hang out with a whole gang of pretty cool ectoplasmic peeps—and one coonhound named Duke. His master loved him so much, the faithful dog was laid to rest in the family plot and now gallops through the graveyard after sundown, usually chasing a ghostly tennis ball thrown by a Confederate colonel.

(No, I don't know how a tennis ball becomes a ghost. Focus, people.)

The officer in question, Colonel Beauregard T. Longworth, functions as something of a graveyard governor. The tall, dignified old soldier says he must remain at his "post" until the South rises again, so basically, he won't be going anywhere anytime soon.

As far as I can tell, that's a matter of individual choice, but truth be told, Beau couldn't leave the cemetery even if he wanted to. He and all the other spirits in residence are contained by an invisible barrier so strong that if I'm outside the graveyard fence, I can't see the ghosts on the inside or even hear their voices.

Jeff Kirk, a Briar Hollow High football star killed in a bus crash on a mountain road in 1956, demonstrated this fact for Tori and me on our first visit. He charged the fence, attempting to launch himself over the barrier, only to run smack into a transparent, but very solid surface that threw him backwards.

(Thankfully, they buried Jeff with his helmet.)

When Tori and I subsequently found ourselves smack in the middle of a series of unsolved murders, Beau and the other ghosts helped us, in part because one of the victims is a graveyard resident.

Not helping the spirits by doing something for them in return didn't feel right, so I started researching ways to release them. Since all of my powers have come in spontaneously, doing some kind of spell or ritual or something along those lines felt beyond daunting, hence the crash course in Being a Witch 101.

Oh. Wait. I haven't told you what I can do besides talk to ghosts.

So far, I can move objects with my mind. That one is called telekinesis.

Also, if I touch something and sort of clear my thoughts, I can get images and memories associated with the object. That's psychometry. I can pretty much control when it happens, so it's not like I'm a witchy version of that chick Rogue from the X-Men comics having to wear gloves all the time.

(Sorry. My high school boyfriend, Billy Wayne, was a major geek. To him, visiting Comic Con was like taking a pilgrimage to the Holy Land.)

Aunt Fiona has led me to believe there will be more abilities, especially if I make an effort to get up to speed, which is something I've also been working on.

For instance, the store stocks herbs and crystals, so I've spent a lot of time learning the properties attributed to each. In fact, I've started carrying a piece of amethyst in my pocket for "change, protection, and enlightenment." I have more than enough of the first, and could use a healthy dose of two and three.

Dispensing herbs and recommending teas or infusions is more like practicing folk medicine than performing actual magic. Aunt Fiona had a slate of standing orders for regular customers that I simply continue to fill. For new-comers, I err on the side of caution. Chamomile to cure insomnia, shaggy hickory bark for coughs—that kind of thing.

But doing something to help the cemetery ghosts was incredibly more complicated and potentially risky. For instance, necromancy was totally out. That's magic to raise

the dead. The last thing I wanted to do was create a hoard
of *Walking Dead* extras.

And the ritual involves a goat.

You don't want to know.

After hours of research, I thought I might be dealing
with some kind of binding spell. But why would someone
do that? According to Beau, Aunt Fiona helped a couple
of spirits to "move on," but even she hadn't been able to
lift the barrier at the periphery of the property for them
all.

She thought the reason was that the ghosts had unfinished business in this plane of existence, but I wasn't so
sure about that. It just sounded a little too easy and pat for
me, like a leftover script they didn't get to shoot before
Ghost Whisperer was canceled.

But I had already come up with a nagging question of
my own. Who put the spell on the cemetery in the first
place and why? From what I could tell, no one buried in
the graveyard presented any possible danger to anyone
living or dead.

Have you caught on to the second nagging question?

For a spell to be cast, you need a witch.

Were there other witches in Briar Hollow?

And, to blatantly steal a line, were they good witches
or bad witches?

Was I getting ready to play the new girl in town on an
episode of *The Real Witches of Briar Hollow*?

I would have loved to discuss all this with Aunt Fiona,
but she's not easy to track down on the other side. All I
know is there's a bowling league and something called
"Punk That Ouija Board."

When my magical research stalled at that point, I
decided to try to find out more about the cemetery itself.
Briar Hollow is located in the northeast corner of North
Carolina, adjacent to the Blue Ridge Parkway.

In this part of Appalachia, there are three major cultural groups that comprise the heritage of the mountain people: Scot-Irish settlers from Europe, the native Cherokee people, and the descendants of African slaves.

Each of those cultures offers up a rich and unique body of folklore and mythology. I had never taken the time to learn anything about what is popularly known as "Appalachian granny magic," because frankly I had no reason to.

Now that I do have a reason, I'm more than a little ashamed about my ignorance of the region where I was born and raised. And trust me, I still have a lot to learn.

After everything was settled about the unsolved murders, I began to sit up night after night watching living history interviews on YouTube that recorded for posterity the lives of remarkable mountain women. They talked about the old days up in the hills, before the Great Depression and even earlier.

Those were the days when money had no meaning and people lived by the barter system. By modern standards, we would call those people poor, and even backward, but I was moved to tears by the daughter of a Cherokee healer who told an interviewer in 1995 that she no longer had anything to be happy about.

For her, the hard times were the best years of her life. I'm still working on getting my head wrapped around that lesson, but I think it's safe to say a major part of it is, we have things too easy.

When I inherited the store, I didn't expect to learn such a fundamental truth about who I am. Aunt Fiona told me that she trusted me with her magic because she knew in the depths of my heart I always know the right thing to do. I'm not so sure about that, but I was convinced that helping the spirits in the cemetery was one of those "right" things.

The problem with doing the right thing is that sometimes you have to get there by the wrong road. That night, while Tori and the cats snored on the couch, I picked a wrong road right through the Orkney Islands.

For those of you for whom high school geography is but a dim memory, the Orkney Islands sit off the northeast coast of Scotland. The people who live there are 25% Norwegian. Their mythology and folklore derive from both Celtic and Norse traditions. Historians have documented a particular fear among the Orkney Islanders of the dead rising from the grave to torment the living.

(And you thought worrying about the zombie apocalypse was a modern phenomenon.)

Because of that fear, and against all recognized Christian doctrine, the Islanders made use of binding rituals to keep the dead well and truly planted in the earth.

I know all of this because I acquired a list of everyone buried in the local cemetery. One name jumped out at me, Knasgowa Skea. The first name is Cherokee for "Heron." The surname is from the Orkney Islands and is taken from the Gaelic word "shee," which is a fairy hill.

In these parts it wasn't unusual for a Scot-Irish man to marry an Indian woman. So much so, that folks who identify themselves in the United States as Native Americans may also have applied for and received membership in their clan back in Scotland. Specifically, this cultural mix is referred to as Scoto-Indian.

What caught my eye, however, was that last name. I was looking for anything in the cemetery that had a magical connection. First, I started looking into fairies, and I'm here to tell you that they are not cute little winged creatures like Tinkerbell. They're nasty sword-carrying mini warriors with bad dispositions, and you seriously do not want to tangle with them.

In the process of doing that reading, however, I ran

across the Cherokee legend of the Little People. According to the Cherokee, the Little People are a race of kindly, gentle, music-loving spirits who stand about two feet tall. They wear their hair so long that it touches the ground, and they make their homes in rock caves on mountainsides.

According to the Cherokee, there are really three types of Little People: Laurel, Rock, and Dogwood. The Laurel People are mischief-makers. Among other things, they are responsible for children laughing in their sleep. Rock People, on the other hand, are known for getting even for invasions of their territory by stealing children. Finally, there are the Dogwood People. They are the ones with the reputation for being kind and caring.

Now, here's where it gets interesting.

When Scots came to the United States and heard the Cherokee legends of the Little People, they assumed the Indians were talking about brownies, small creatures in Gaelic legend that like to live in close association with households.

Brownies are particularly fond of doing helpful little chores in exchange for porridge and honey, but they don't like to be seen. Therefore, their good works are done by dark of night.

I'm just going out on a limb here, but I think J.K. Rowling based her house elves on brownies. To be 100% truthful? I really don't care about the exact genealogy of little magical creatures with a desire to clean my house. If you exist, you are totally welcome. Seriously, any house elves reading this? Come on over! You can have all the porridge and honey you want.

The way I'm talking here, I'm making it sound like I went into the situation armed with all kinds of knowledge. I assure you that that was not the case. Which may have been part of the problem.

That night, after the argument with Myrtle about the

paint, everything that I'm telling you now was scrawled over a series of notebooks, and contained in random web pages saved on my laptop.

Maybe it was the red wine and popcorn, but I couldn't sleep that night, and suddenly I looked at all these random pieces of information, and they started to not look so random at all.

I realized that there was a Cherokee woman who had been married to a Scotsman from the Orkney Islands buried in a cemetery where none of the spirits of the dead could move on.

As far as the tradition of the Little People and the brownies, all it meant to me at the time was that the Scots and the Cherokees shared a lot of similar folklore.

My working theory was that Knasgowa's husband might have decided to bind her to her grave just to be safe, and did his job entirely too well.

When I turned out the light that night I was feeling pretty satisfied with myself. Actually, let me rephrase that with language my mother would use. I had a swelled head and was getting entirely too big for my britches.

There is nothing worse than a completely ignorant person operating with complete conviction. That night I was thoroughly guilty on both counts, and I couldn't wait to get up the next day and compound the error of my ways, starting with telling Tori everything I just told you.

THREE

Tori stared at me bleary eyed over the breakfast table while the cats scarfed down their morning chow. She took another hit of her coffee liberally laced with half-and-half and said, "So, you think a Scottish-Indian Elf on the Shelf locked the cemetery gate and hid the key?" she asked.

Not exactly how I would have summarized the careful recitation of relevant folklore and mythology I had just shared with her, but close enough.

"More or less," I admitted.

"And we're going to, what, give the elf socks, set it free, and hope Voldemort doesn't find out?"

(Tori had read all the *Harry Potter* books. Twice.)

"I kind of doubt socks had anything to do with Orkney Island binding rituals," I said. "From what I read it was more like stick corn between the dead person's toes and cover the corpse in barley, or something along those lines."

"That would have been my next suggestion," Tori said sardonically. "So, do we have a plan?"

"Well, this is cemetery night," I said. "I thought we might start by finding Knasgowa's grave."

"You don't think she's there hanging out with the others?" Tori asked, reaching for another piece of toast.

"I can't be certain," I said, "but I haven't seen anyone there who looks like a little old Cherokee woman. According to the list I got from the Briar Hollow Historical Society, she was 85 when she died."

Tori frowned. "And her husband was still alive?"

"Alexander Skea lived to be 98," I said.

"And I'll bet he was just a joy to be around," Tori grumbled.

"Okay," I said, "you need another cup of coffee. Maybe two. You cannot go downstairs and be in a bad mood with Myrtle. We need those cabinets moved today."

"I'm not upset with Myrtle anymore," Tori said. "Yule snored in my ear all night and Xavier hogged the pillow."

"Welcome to my world," I said, smothering a smile. "Mark says your new mini apartment will be ready in another 2 or 3 days. Isn't your furniture supposed to be delivered Saturday?"

"It is," Tori said, brightening up. "I can hardly wait to play with it."

The addition on the back of the shop was less than 400 sq. ft. Tori had opted for a Murphy bed to save space, and then had gone shopping for multi-purpose furniture. She'd picked out a lot of cool pieces, including a coffee table that housed four chairs in its base and became taller at the touch of a hidden hydraulic switch.

I was fascinated with her tiny kitchen that included a two-burner stove and a microwave / convection oven combo, as well as an all-in-one washer-drier. The whole electrical system interfaced with her smartphone and nothing but LED bulbs were allowed over the threshold.

Tori had been talking for years about saving her money to build a tiny home, but I hadn't realized how much she'd been able to put away, or how inexpensive a small, efficient space could really be. Honestly, I was a little jealous.

In the interest of privacy, there were two entrances to the apartment; one into the store and another into the alley where we parked our cars under a newly constructed double carport. Owning your own building has major advantages when it comes time to get building permits. Other than having to move the meters closer to the alley, everything was going smoothly under Mark's careful supervision.

And, speaking of things going smoothly, when Tori and I went downstairs, we found a grim-faced contractor with a crowbar in his hand staring at the recalcitrant wall cabinets.

"Good morning," Mark said in a resigned tone.

Tori and I both offered our good mornings, and then I said to Mark, "You look like you're about to enter battle."

"I feel like I am," he admitted, "but it's killing me that to win I have to ruin these antiques."

"Maybe that won't be necessary," I said. "Why don't you try to move them one more time?"

Mark shook his head doubtfully. "Okay," he said. "It won't do any good, but we'll try."

He motioned to his workers, who positioned themselves on either side of the first cabinet. It slid away from the wall like butter on a hot pancake.

Mark turned to me in astonishment. "Okay," he demanded, "what did you do to them?"

"Me?" I said. "How in the world could I have done anything? I think you all just loosened them up yesterday."

Trust me. That one always works on men.

"Huh," Mark grunted. "Maybe. Come on, guys. Let's just get these things across the room before they decide to get stuck to the wall again."

We left the men to their work. Tori headed down to George and Irma's grocery on the corner to pick up her latest order of coffee beans. (More on that in a minute.) I went into the storeroom to feed Rodney, our resident rodent.

Yes, Aunt Fiona also left me a rat—a handsome black-

and-white rat to be precise. Rodney lives in a premium condo behind two cans of horse liniment on a back shelf in the storeroom, an area Tori now calls the Rat Cave.

I don't know why that arrangement suits Rodney, but when I asked if he'd like his quarters to be moved to a location with a better view, he answered with a vehement negative shake of his head. There's no accounting for someone's taste in real estate.

Even though Mark and the guys were making plenty of noise out in the main room, I kept my voice low when I said, "Thank you, Myrtle. I really appreciate you letting them move the cabinets."

In response, I heard a subdued musical chime that sounded like, "Don't mention it."

So far the day was getting off to a good start.

At the sound of my voice, Rodney came scampering out to the edge of his shelf, and gave me a wave with one front paw.

"Good morning, Rodney," I said. "Sorry I'm a little late today. Ready for your breakfast?"

Talk about the great granddaddy of all rhetorical questions. Rodney is always ready for a meal any time of the day, and has proven himself to be an accomplished albeit polite beggar.

He would prefer a steady diet of junk food, but now that I'm in charge of his menu, Rodney eats at least one meal a day of premium, nutritionally balanced, rodent chow. My own mother has always said that breakfast is the most important meal of the day, so that's when Rodney gets his health food.

At the sound of the pellets bouncing off of his bowl, Rodney made a face. It's difficult to describe how a rat can grimace in displeasure, but trust me, Rodney pulls it off.

"Quit your complaining," I scolded. "Since I insisted you start eating some decent food, you're getting yourself a real six pack. You're going to have to beat the lady rats off with a stick."

In reply to that, Rodney stood up on his hind legs and raised his front legs in a classic bodybuilder stance. When he was sure I was looking at him, Rodney flexed his muscles.

"That's more like it," I said, putting his bowl down. The rat stared at the pellets for a minute and then started munching with studied resignation.

Rodney is yet another of the many mysteries of Aunt Fiona's store. According to Chase, the domestic rat was left at the front door of the shop in his cage. There has to be more to the story than that. Rodney has an uncanny degree of intelligence and personality. He's not just any rat, but so far he hasn't come clean about the truth of his origins.

I sat down in the worn-out easy chair that was my favorite and opened my iPad to look at the day's news. It wasn't long before Tori came in carrying two big boxes along with a white paper bag of donut holes balanced on top.

"My God, Tori," I said, getting up to rescue the bag, "we just had breakfast."

"And now we will have second breakfast," she grinned.

(She's also seen all the *Lord of the Rings* movies. More than twice.)

For the time being, Irma at the corner grocery was lumping Tori's experimental coffee bean purchases in with her own orders to save us shipping costs. Before my very eyes, my bestie, who used to consider putting peanuts in her soda pop a delicacy, was turning into a coffee aficionado.

As I watched Tori unpacking sacks of beans, she asked brightly, "So what's the plan for today?"

Inwardly, I groaned and steeled myself for what was to come.

"First, I think we should re-stock those cabinets the guys just moved," I said, with equal good cheer, "and then we really do have to decide on an espresso machine."

It was Tori's turn to groan—audibly.

For weeks we'd gone back and forth on this very question. I was in favor of going with a used machine to save a little money and Tori was adamant that we not risk "the potential for the god shot."

Let me be real honest here. After 11 years of working at Tom's Cafe, I can tell you how long a pot of coffee has been sitting on the burner, but I wouldn't know Kopi Luwak from Folgers, and I had never even heard of the god shot until Tori stopped speaking English and started talking barista.

Let's work through this foreign language one step at a time, starting with Kopi Luwak.

Considered the elite of the coffee elite, Kopi Luwak costs upwards of $700 per kilogram. If you flunked the metric system like I did, a kilogram is 2.2 pounds. I guess that makes $350 a pound a bargain in some people's books, but it's freaking outrageous as far as I'm concerned and we sure as heck won't be carrying the stuff.

You know why?

The beans are "partially digested" by some jungle civet cat.

What does "partially digested" mean?

Think "litter box harvest" and you'll be on the right page.

Do I even need to say, "gross?"

Then there's this matter of the god shot, which has become Tori's personal goal in life. Apparently, baristas the world over dream and strategize about finding this particular Holy Grail.

The first step in the universal strategy to achieve the god shot?

Select the right espresso machine.

Hence, weeks of discussion during which my frugality ran head-on into Tori's new obsession. If I caved on this subject, she would buy a machine that cost more than her new apartment behind the shop.

When showing me endless online catalog pages didn't further her case, Tori sent off for literally dozens of brochures, which now littered the coffee table (ironic, right?) in the Rat Cave.

"Jinksy," she said, "I really don't want to have this argument with you again."

Tori and I almost never argue, and the only really serious fight we ever had was over two losers we were dating named Cody and Jesse.

"We're not arguing," I countered, "we're discussing. Could we just come down from the $20,000 price point and look at some more . . . economical . . . choices?"

"You mean like the machine on Craigslist that has been sludging out motor oil shots in some dive called Bennie's Beans and Bait?" she asked defensively.

(Bear with me, there is a point to all this coffee talk.)

Sighing, I said, "Okay. Granted, the Yelp reviews on Bennie's have moved me off that idea."

Bennie's ad for the used espresso machine read, "Asking $50 or best offer. Would consider a trade for primo fishing tackle."

Inwardly gulping, I said, in the spirit of compromise, "Could you live with something in the $1,000 to $3,000 range?"

We were more than splitting the price of the equipment, but I was still majorly falling on my sword with that offer.

Tori's eyes lit up. "You mean it?" she asked excitedly.

"Yes," I said, still feeling a little sick at my stomach. "I mean it."

"How about I grind some of these Ethiopia Konga single estate beans for the French press and we'll look at the brochures again?"

See what I mean? English is no longer spoken here.

I will, however, concede that until Tori made coffee for me in a French press, I never knew such a thing existed, which means I had led a deprived life. Best way to make coffee *ever*.

"Deal," I said, "but no hogging the donut holes."

We spent the rest of the morning narrowing down our choices until I gave Tori the go ahead to place a call to New York and get a La Pavoni machine (in red, no less, and, thankfully, on sale) headed our way.

Just before she hit the "send" button, Tori looked up at the ceiling and said, "You okay with this, Myrtle?"

The question was instantly rewarded with a shower of gold stars, which made me breathe a sigh of relief.

Mutiny on the playground avoided for one more morning.

FOUR

That night at the cemetery, Jeff, the high school football player, was waiting for us when we came through the gate. "Hi, Tori! Hi, Jinx!" he said, in an excited voice. "Did you bring it?"

"It" was the latest issue of *Sports Illustrated*. Jeff couldn't turn the pages by himself, but Tori was happy to read the magazine with him and to answer his questions. I'm completely lacking the sports gene, but she inherited a double dose. Her parents, Gemma and Howard, are possibly the two most embarrassing people you'd never want to sit with at a football game.

Tori shot me a questioning look. "Go ahead," I said. "I want to talk to Colonel Longworth."

I found the old soldier near his white marble obelisk. "Good evening, Miss Jinx," Beau said, bowing gallantly. "Forgive me for not being at the cemetery entrance to greet you. I was detained on a matter of diplomatic importance."

"That's okay, Beau," I said. "Everything okay?"

"Okay" being a relative term to a guy who had been dead since the Civil War.

Beau sighed. "Yes," he said wearily. "I was merely mediating a dispute between Mrs. Walters and Miss Lou Ella."

Mrs. Walters was a sweet 19th century granny laid to

rest in her best blue gingham dress and Miss Lou Ella was a 1960s-era hairdresser complete with bouffant and rhinestone-encrusted cat's eye glasses.

"Uh-oh," I said, "what happened?"

"I am afraid Miss Lou Ella was telling stories of her exploits with single young gentlemen that extended far beyond the acceptable morals of Mrs. Walter's time," he said. "An unfortunate discussion of a religious nature ensued, and Mrs. Walters used some rather harsh words relative to Miss Lou Ella's morality."

That's a really long way to get around to saying Mrs. Walters probably politely called Miss Lou Ella a slut.

"And how did this cat fight play out?" I asked.

"There was a great deal of unnecessary wind and some shrieking," he said, "precisely the sort of thing that the living expect of a haunted graveyard. Thankfully there were no witnesses, but I really cannot allow that kind of behavior to go unchecked. It will disrupt the peaceful nature of our community."

"You really are a sort of mayor out here, aren't you?" I said.

"I think it's simply the effect of the uniform," Longworth said modestly.

That was my opening. "Given your knowledge of everyone who lives . . . er, resides here," I said, "can you help me locate a grave?"

"Of course," Longworth said. "Whose final resting place are you seeking?"

"A Cherokee woman named Knasgowa Skea," I said.

Beau hesitated, and then said, "I do know the location of this woman's grave, but if it is not too presumptuous of me, may I ask the nature of your interest in her?"

That I wasn't expecting.

"I think she may be the key to why all of you are trapped inside the fence," I explained. "Her husband,

Alexander Skea, was born in the Orkney Islands. I've discovered that their folklore contains some unusual beliefs about the dead rising to torment the living. If I'm right, Alexander may have put some kind of spell on his wife's grave to bind her to that spot, and it worked too well."

"An interesting theory," the Colonel said. "Most of the spirits here do not care to go near Mrs. Skea's grave."

"Why?" I asked.

Beau seemed to be searching for the right words. "There is a certain . . . energy associated with her resting place," he said finally. "The others find it uncomfortable."

"And you, sir?"

"I am aware of the sensation," he admitted, "but it isn't sufficient to drive me away. If you are determined to see her grave, I am capable of taking you there. Shall we?"

With those words, the Colonel offered me his arm. The gesture was already an old game between us. All of the spirits in the graveyard appeared to me in much the same way, like images off an old black-and-white TV set. For some of them that analogy extends to wavy lines and static.

Of all the ghosts, Colonel Longworth's "signal" is the strongest. I can see him clearly, but I can't touch him. I certainly can't take his arm, but it makes him feel better to offer it, so I smiled, and said, "Thank you, kind sir," and fell in beside him. As we walked, I held my left arm against my waist to make the illusion more real for the courtly old officer.

Beau took me to the exact center of the graveyard. We stopped at a black marble marker, which must have been both expensive and unusual in its day. The inscription read, *Knasgowa, wife of Alexander, daughter of the Cherokee Nation.*

Turning to me, Beau asked, "Do you feel it?"

Thanks to the work I'd put into controlling my psychometry by that time, I had already taught myself to empty my thoughts and reach out with my mind. When I did, I encountered a kind of . . . blankness over the grave, almost as if the air itself was dead.

I frowned and turned to Beau. "I don't get it," I said. "The other graves don't feel like this."

"Precisely," Beau said. "To us it feels like a void into which none of us wish to fall."

"I can sure understand why," I said. "Maybe that's the effect of the binding spell. Did Aunt Fiona know about this?"

"Miss Fiona did know," the Colonel said cryptically.

I waited, but when Beau said nothing more, I had to prod him. "*And*?" I asked.

"Your aunt said that what is connected to this grave should not be released," the old man replied. "Perhaps you should heed her warning."

This would be the part where I should have clued in that if Aunt Fiona said leave it alone, my next move was to back away. Unfortunately, the last time I talked to my aunt, she told me that I possessed powers that were stronger than her own, and, as much as I hate to admit it, I let that go straight to my head.

"I've done a lot of research into this topic of binding the dead," I told Beau. "I think I can handle this."

Right. Of course you can—armed with a high school diploma, 11 years of experience waiting tables, about a month of being a witch, and Google.

Hi, my name is Jinx, and I'm an egocentric idiot.

Just then, Tori walked up to join us, and I saw a funny look come over her face. "Whoa," she said, "this place gives me the heebie jeebies. What's up with that?"

"This is Knasgowa's grave," I said. "According to the Colonel, all the spirits in the cemetery feel the same way about her plot that you do."

"So we abort, right?" Tori said.

That would be the voice of reason, which I was about to blithely ignore.

"No," I said. "I think you're all just feeling the binding spell, which I'm going to try to turn off." Reaching in my pocket, I pulled out a crinkled piece of paper.

"What's that?" Tori asked, justifiable suspicion dripping off every syllable.

"It's a spell to release a trapped ghost," I said confidently. "I edited it a little bit so it will work on the binding spell."

Note that I just leveled up there on the egocentrism thing.

"Now hang on," Tori said. "We need to talk about this for a minute. You *edited* the spell?"

"Yeah. So what?"

"And where did you find this spell in the first place?" Tori asked.

I felt the heat rise to my face. "It was on a Wiccan website."

"A real Wiccan website?"

"Um," I hedged, "she *said* she's a Wiccan sole practitioner."

"And Miss I Make Up My Own Rules got this spell where exactly?" Tori asked, refusing to give up.

"Uh, from a voodoo wiki."

Have I mentioned that Tori has an uncanny ability to summarize my bad ideas? Case in point, listen to what she said next. I should have. Listened, that is.

"In what alternate universe is it a good idea to use an edited voodoo quasi-Wicca spell to release a Cherokee woman bound to her grave by some Orkney Scot dude?" Tori demanded. "I may not be an expert, Jinksy, but mixing magic has to be like mixing your booze. A really bad idea with a *way* worse hangover."

At this juncture, I should have remembered that Tori

was the one who told me not to mix sloe gin with Southern Comfort and Diet Dr. Pepper when we were in high school. She was also the person who held my hair later when I was calling Ralph.

But no, my memory failed me, and I heard myself saying emphatically, "I think I know what I'm doing."

To Tori's credit, she didn't tell me to get over myself, but she did suggest that both she and Colonel Longworth back a long way off while I threw myself straight over a magical cliff.

When she was several yards away, Tori turned and looked back at me. "Don't blow yourself up or anything, Jinksy," she called out, in a worried tone. "I'm kind of used to having you around."

That was the first time I felt a glimmer of doubt. I was kind of used to being around, but hey, in for a dime, in for a dollar. Ever heard of something called inflation?

If I had really done as much homework as I claimed to have done, I would have cast a protective circle around the grave before I read the spell. That would have contained any spirits that I happened to wake up. But I didn't do that.

Instead, I cleared my mind and started reading what was on the paper, trying to channel my inner energies outward, as the website had instructed me to do.

Nothing happened.

So, genius here, read the spell again.

Nothing happened.

Ever heard of a little game played at slumber parties with mirrors called Bloody Mary?

I read the spell again.

And promptly found out the real meaning of the phrase, "Three's the charm."

FIVE

What happened next is a whole lot harder to explain. A transparent column of energy rose from Knasgowa's grave. It mushroomed at the top like water overflowing a glass, and then melted outward, rushing to cover the entire cemetery. The wave passed over me like thick, hot molasses. The barrier at the fence caught and contained the onslaught, but the mass pooled at the base, gaining momentum and weight. It felt as if we were standing inside a bubble strained to the brink. Within seconds, the thin shell shattered and energy flowed over the fence and into the night.

Then I heard the voices. All around me spirits rose from their graves, but these were not like the ghosts who had become my friends. These spirits were confused and disoriented, awakened from the deepest slumber of all to stumble into a half reality caught in the void between two worlds.

There was no one there who could help me undo what I had done, but I still turned toward Tori and the Colonel.

"Beau," I pleaded, "do something."

Colonel Beauregard T. Longworth was not a man to shirk the responsibilities of command, even one handed to him amidst the chaos of battle. At the top of his lungs he bellowed, "Silence!"

31

The voices stopped, and all the ghosts turned toward the Colonel.

"Resorting to bedlam will only increase your fears," he said, in a strong, but kind voice. "In life, many of you were friends. Find the people you know and congregate quietly."

To my complete amazement, the spirits began to do as they were told. Many of them looked happy and relieved when they spotted people they knew, raising their hands in hopeful greetings and rushing to stand together, talking quietly amongst themselves.

It was harder to look at the lone spirits, those who searched the crowd and saw no one familiar. They too began to clump together, seeking safety in numbers, but their expressions remained nervous and frightened.

Beau and Tori joined me at the foot of Knasgowa's grave. Speaking to the Colonel, I said, "With leadership skill like that, why exactly did the South lose the war?"

"Gallantry in the face of fire was not the deficit of the Southern cause," Beau said grimly. "Our issues rose in equal parts from Yankee perfidy and a rather deplorable lack of an industrial base."

I wasn't sure what "perfidy" meant, but I was betting it wasn't a compliment.

"Guess your Mocha Mojo Magic cocktail worked there, Jinksy," Tori said, giving me a look that was an odd mixture of admiration and horror. "Now what the heck are we supposed to do?"

A slight movement behind Knasgowa's tombstone caught my eye. "Who's back there?" I demanded.

A small face peered apprehensively around the edge of the black marble. "Please, Great Sorceress, your humble minion means you no harm."

Humble minion? This was not sounding good. At all.

"Step out here so we can see you," I said.

At first I thought the figure that emerged from the shadows was a child, but the shy, smiling face was that of an old man. He couldn't have been more than two feet tall.

In spite of my shock, I smiled back. "Who are you?" I asked.

I wanted to say *"what* are you," but that seemed incredibly rude.

The name he gave us contained every syllable in the alphabet—twice—and ended with what sounded a lot like a cat hacking a hairball.

We all hesitated awkwardly, and then Tori came to the rescue.

"How about we just call you Darby?" she suggested.

Our moms are both old movie freaks. I knew instantly what she meant. *Darby O'Gill and the Little People.* Disney, circa 1959. Think leprechauns.

The little man turned to me. "Mistress, do you wish that I answer to this name?" he asked.

Okay. "Mistress" was a marginal improvement over "great sorceress," but I was still a little uncomfortable with all the metaphysical honorifics.

"Yes," I said, "it would be a lot easier for us to call you Darby. If you don't mind my asking, why do you keep calling *me* 'mistress'?"

To my acute embarrassment, Darby actually went down on one knee and bowed his head when he answered.

"You are the Great Sorceress who freed me from my prison," he said, in a humble and reverent tone. "I will serve you faithfully for the rest of my life, Mistress."

Oh, God.

"Darby, *please,* stand up," I said, trying to be both emphatic and appreciative at the same time. "You don't need to do that kneeling thing again—*ever.*"

"As you wish, Mistress," he said, standing up to his full, minuscule height.

"My name is Jinx," I said. "Use it."

The little guy's eyes lit up like I had just handed him a huge, wrapped package. "Thank you, Mistress Jinx, for allowing me the privilege of speaking your name," he gushed. "I am deeply honored."

Beside me I heard Tori snicker. I shot her a murderous side-glance. By this time, I was completely over my etiquette angst.

"Darby," I said, "I don't mean to be rude, but *what* are you exactly?"

"My kind are known by many names," he said.

So not helpful.

I turned to Beau. "Any ideas, Colonel?"

"The native peoples of this region, the Cherokee, had many legends regarding little people who were supposed to live in the deep woods," he answered. "You did just attempt a work of magic over the grave of a woman of that tribe."

Give the old dead Confederate dude a prize.

"Darby, did you know Knasgowa Skea?" I asked.

Tears pooled in the little man's eyes.

"She was my master's wife," he said. "Mistress Skea was very kind to me."

"You . . . uh . . . served, Alexander Skea?" I asked.

Darby attempted to stand up even taller, although that wasn't really possible.

"Like generations of my kind before me," he said proudly, "I was in service to the House of Skea. Master Alexander brought me with him when he came to the New World."

Now we were starting to get somewhere.

"If you'll pardon me for bringing this up, Darby," I said, "you're kind of *noticeable*. What did your master tell people about you? I mean, how did he explain you being so... *short*?"

I could have added "and old," but you don't want to hit a guy with too many below-the-belt blows at one time.

Darby's eyes widened. "You do not know of my people, Mistress Jinx?"

"No," I said, as patiently as I could manage, because he was being incredibly slow on the uptake. "I don't know anything about your kind."

As soon as the words were out of my mouth, Darby was gone.

"What the *heck* was *that*?" Tori said. "And where did he go?"

"I am here," Darby's voice said out of thin air.

Oh, just freaking great. An *invisible* minion. This was just getting better by the minute. *Not.*

"Uh, okay," I said. "Got it. Now stop doing . . . that."

At my command, Darby was standing in front of us again.

"You have to admit that's a pretty neat trick, Jinksy," Tori said.

"Indeed," Colonel Longworth agreed. "It would have certainly given my troops a tactical advantage."

They so were not helping.

"Darby," I said, "why are you here?"

"When Master Alexander bound his wife to her grave, he bound me as well," Darby said. "It has been my job these many years to stand guard over her final resting place, but your magic has freed me, and my obligation to Master Alexander has been severed. I now serve you."

Colonel Longworth cleared his throat.

"If I may?" he asked.

"By all means," I said. "Be my guest."

Beau got down on one knee to look Darby in the eye. It didn't work. The Colonel still towered over the tiny creature.

"Darby, in what year did you accompany your master to these shores?" Beau asked.

"The year of our Lord seventeen hundred and eighty six," Darby answered brightly.

The date on the gravestone was 1853. Darby had been at his post for 162 years.

"Uh, question?" Tori said, holding her hand up like the total geek she can be sometimes.

"Sure," I said, "you might as well get in this game, too."

"Where's Alexander?" she asked.

"Huh?" I said.

"This is a single grave," she said, pointing at the black granite marker. "You told me Alexander Skea lived to be 98. Where's he buried?"

"Any ideas, Darby?" I asked.

"No, Mistress Jinx," the little man said. "I have not seen my master since the night of my mistress' burial."

Beau, still down on the same level with Darby, asked, "How old was your master when he came to this land?"

"Master Alexander had reached the age of 20 years when he booked passage for the New World," Darby answered.

I did the mental math. "Alexander died in 1864," I said.

"During the Late Unpleasantness," Beau said, getting back to his feet.

For those of you who need it, let me offer a translation. "Late Unpleasantness" is southern for "Civil War." You'll also hear it called the "War of Northern Aggression." My Yankee friends just *love* that one.

"True," I said, "but a 98-year-old man was hardly fighting for the southern cause, Beau."

The old soldier shook his head. "In the closing years of the war, Miss Jinx, the South called upon all her native sons. I had boys as young as 12 years under my command, and a veteran of the War of 1812 who, though well into his dotage, could still shoulder a rifle."

Before we could talk any more about Alexander Skea, the sound of someone clearing their throat made all of us turn around. There were three ghosts standing behind us, all in their best Sunday suits. The one who was apparently in charge stepped forward.

"My name is Howard McAlpin," he barked. "I'm the mayor of Briar Hollow and I demand to know what's going on here."

Wow. Was he ever getting ready to learn the true meaning of "term limits."

"Uh, hi," I said, adding hastily, "Mr. Mayor."

"Who are you, young woman?" Mayor McAlpin demanded. "Why are we all out here in the cemetery in the middle of the night?"

"Okay, well, yeah," I hedged. "That's kind of a long story. You see, sir . . ."

My voice trailed off and I looked at Tori, appealing for help.

"Just tell him," she said. "They're going to have to know sooner or later."

Gathering my courage, I turned back to McAlpin, and said, "You're in the cemetery, sir, because you're dead."

To my complete astonishment, the Mayor burst out laughing. "Oh, that's a good one," he chuckled. "What is this, some kind of Lodge prank? You just wait until I get a hold of those guys. I hope they paid you well."

"No, sir. Really," I said. Trying again, "You're *dead*. I can show you your tombstone."

Out of the corner of my mouth, I whispered desperately in Beau's direction, "We can do that, right?"

"Of course," the Colonel said, in the genial tone of a host. "Gentlemen, if you will follow me."

The three men exchanged bemused glances and fell in behind Beau.

"Great costume there, buddy," McAlpin said as we

walked. "You a Civil War re-enactor or something?"

With great forbearance, Colonel Longworth replied, "I assure you, sir, that my initial experience of the war was quite sufficient. I have no desire to re-enact the conflict."

McAlpin let out a loud guffaw. "You really stay in character," he said, trying to clap Beau on the shoulder. When his hand passed straight through the colonel, an odd, uneasy look came over the politician's face. "How the heck do you do *that*?" he asked.

"Um, Howard?" I said, swiping my hand through his arm, hoping that visuals would help this guy get a clue.

The mayor stared for a second, and then said, "Wow! You guys are good! You should be doing special effects for the movies."

Dumb as a sack of hammers or King of the River Denial? Your pick.

Beau stopped by a modest granite marker and pointed. "Your final resting place, Mr. Mayor."

McAlpin looked down, and scoffed, "Nice try! You think I'm gonna fall for a cheap, gag tombstone made of Styrofoam? Especially one that isn't even big enough for a man of my political stature?"

He made a move to kick the marker. His foot passed completely through the stone, and the mayor lost his balance. Under normal circumstances, he would have fallen on his backside. This time, he floated.

His two lackeys, who, as it turns out, were former Briar Hollow City Councilmen, both backed up and exchanged one of those "you tell him, no *you* do it" looks.

The taller of the two must have drawn the short straw, because he said uneasily, "Howard, I think the dead thing might be a plausible theory."

McAlpin looked at Beau. "You seem to be the one in charge around here," he growled, "so tell me how the heck I get down from here."

Smothering a smile, the Colonel said, "Make a motion as if you were rising from a seated position."

The Russian judge would have given the move low marks, but Howard McAlpin wound up back on his feet. He took a minute to collect itself, and then demanded, "How did this happen?"

"Dude, *really*?" Tori said. "You croaked. Your heart stopped beating. You took the big dirt nap. Get *over* it already."

That's when we found out that we were dealing with a man willing to grasp at any straw that would give him a potential advantage.

"Is that possible?" McAlpin asked eagerly. "Can I get over being dead?"

Okay, that answers the question. Dumber than a sack of hammers.

"I don't think so, sir," I said.

"Well . . . well . . . well," McAlpin stammered, "how did this happen to *me*?"

Ignoring the fact that in life, he had plainly considered himself to be above ultimately dying like the rest of us, I glanced down at the marker. The mayor died in 1983, three years before I was born.

"I have no idea, sir," I said truthfully. Then I added, "You know what they say, you can't avoid death and taxes."

"You most certainly can avoid taxes," he muttered absently. Then, regaining his former bluster, he said in a huff, "I certainly intend to get to the bottom of this."

Not a problem. Dig down about six feet.

As we watched, Howard McAlpin turned on his spectral heel and marched toward the cemetery gate with his own minions following reluctantly behind.

"Dead men walking," Tori muttered, as we took off after them.

"Mr. Mayor," I said, "you really should stay here with Colonel Longworth and the others until I can figure out how to put you back."

That stopped McAlpin in his tracks. "What do you mean put me *back*? You mean in the grave?"

Is there any diplomatic way to tell an outraged ghost he really needs to get back in his casket and stay there?

"Yes, sir," I said, "I didn't intend to raise any of you." As I spoke, I gestured to the grounds around us.

We were surrounded by clumps of ghosts who had already formed several sort of afterlife neighborhood associations. The spirits who recognized each other were congregated in tight clumps, while the regulars, with no prompting from Beau, were circulating among them trying to offer the newcomers some comfort.

When I looked at the frightened and confused faces, I felt sick to my stomach. What had I done? And how was I going to fix it?

"I don't care what your intentions were," McAlpin said. "All the rest of these people can lie back down in their graves if they want to, but I have a town to run."

With that, he stomped right through the cemetery gate and started toward town. After a few steps, however, he stopped and called back to Beau, "Hey! Reenactor guy? Do I have to walk?"

"No," the Colonel replied, "just think about where you want to go."

"Beau!" I said. "Don't help!"

But the admonishment came too late. McAlpin and the two councilmen were gone.

Six

It was almost dawn, and I was never so glad to see the sun coming up. As the first rays pushed over the horizon, the newly awakened spirits began to fade away. "What's happening?" I asked Beau.

"They don't have the strength to appear in daylight," he said. "If you will take note, many of our regulars are also fading. They will return this evening."

That meant that even with the complication of absolutely no sleep, we had about 12 hours to come up with a solution for my major screwup.

"What about you, Beau?" I asked. "You're looking pretty solid to me and you're no longer confined to the cemetery. What are you going to do today?"

The old soldier ducked his head and said, almost shyly, "Miss Jinx, if I give you my word of honor that nothing untoward will occur, may I accompany you to your place of business today? I have long wanted to see the wonders of your modern world."

If any other ghost had asked, I would have given an emphatic "no." But Colonel Longworth was the last person, living or dead, who was ever going to give me any problems.

"It would be my honor to have you spend the day with us, Beau," I said.

He really tried to keep his cool, but the Colonel grinned in spite of himself. "It's been quite some time since I've done anything that could be characterized as . . ." His voice trailed off as he fumbled to find the right word.

"Fun?" Tori suggested mischievously.

"Indeed, Miss Tori," he said. "An aptly chosen descriptive."

In the midst of all the postmortem political posturing staged by Howard McAlpin and his cronies, we'd forgotten about Darby, who had been quietly following us around. Now he spoke up. "If I may, Mistress Jinx," he said, "what will my duties be?"

"Your duties, Darby?" I asked.

"Yes, Mistress," he replied enthusiastically. "I quite enjoy maintaining order in a household and I am exceptionally efficient at gathering information."

I saw Tori's eyes light up at the phrase "order in a household."

"You're a house elf?" she asked brightly.

It was a Harry Potter allusion that promptly went wrong.

Darby grimaced. "I am most certainly *not* an elf," he said, sounding offended. "Elves are completely lacking in discipline. Always running off to cavort around the forest."

Tori processed that for a minute, and then said, "Whoa! Hang on here. Elves really exist?"

"Yes, My Lady," Darby said, "but I implore you to not ask me to deal with them. They are highly unreliable."

"What about fairies?" she asked.

"Also unreliable," Darby said, archly, "and somewhat given to launching military offenses."

Huh. Who would have guessed Tinkerbell was really G.I. Jane?

Tori was on a roll. "So, if you're not an elf and you're not a fairy," she said, "what are you exactly?"

Thank God she asked before I had to.

Squaring his shoulders and puffing out his chest, Darby said, "I am a brownie."

Tori looked at me and grinned. "Guess we should have called him Duncan, huh?" she said.

"If you wish for me to answer to . . ." Darby started.

"No," I said hastily, heading off that train before it reached the crossing of Accommodating and Annoying. "That was a private joke."

When Tori and I get depressed, we mix up multiple batches of brownies. Through the years, we have speculated that we may be single-handedly keeping Duncan Hines in business.

Darby looked confused, but his faithful-minion manners remained perfect. "As you wish, Mistress Jinx," he said obligingly.

"Jinksy," Tori whispered, "we can't take Beau with us and leave the little guy here."

"I know," I whispered back, "but have you forgotten that the shop is currently crawling with workers every day?"

"Have you forgotten Darby is the mini *Invisible Man*?" she shot back.

Actually, I had forgotten.

I turned back to the patiently waiting brownie. "Okay, Darby, we'll figure out what you can do to help out around the shop later, but for now, all I need you to do is stay invisible when other people are around. Can you handle that?"

"Of course, Mistress," Darby said, "but I must have something to do. It is my purpose to serve."

I couldn't fault his work ethic. Then an idea occurred to me.

"You say you're good at getting information?" I asked.

"Yes, Mistress."

"And how's your memory?"

"Perfect, Mistress."

"Then for now, you just watch everything that goes on and remember it all in case I have any questions for you," I said. "Okay?"

"Of course, Mistress," Darby said, inclining his head. "I will not fail you."

We must have made for a ludicrously unlikely quartet leaving the cemetery; two sleepy women, a Confederate Colonel, and a magical little person.

My mind was already on getting an hour or two of sleep before opening the shop, so it didn't occur to me that Colonel Longworth was doing something incredibly epic by walking out the gate.

As soon as his boot crossed the boundary, Beau hesitated.

That's when it dawned on me that something major was taking place.

"Are you okay, Beau?" I asked worriedly. So many things had gone wrong with my misguided attempt to set the cemetery ghosts free, I was scared to death we were in for more.

We were, by the way—in for more—but not right at that moment.

"I am quite unharmed, Miss Jinx," the Colonel said. "It is only that I have long stared beyond the confines of this graveyard and yearned to freely explore the world again. Thank you for setting me free."

Okay, maybe not *everything* had gone wrong with the night's plans.

Although Beau could have simply gotten to the store on his own power, he chose to ride in the car with us. Darby climbed in the back as well, and without being prompted, instantly went invisible.

The long night was starting to wear on me, and Tori

was already half asleep, slumped against the car door. Thankfully it was just a little after six, so hopefully we could get in the store without anyone noticing. If Chase McGregor saw us from the windows of his apartment, I could always concoct some story about going out super early for breakfast. After all, Tori and I were both used to working the morning shift at Tom's and eating on the run while we carried eggs and bacon out to the customers. Besides, Chase is pretty sweet on me. He wouldn't question the story.

The streets were deserted when I turned my cherry-red Prius onto the courthouse square and steered down the narrow alley behind the shop. There is one good thing about driving a hybrid when you're trying for stealth; they're very quiet cars.

I parked under the new carport and we all got out. Well, Tori and I got out. Beau was just suddenly standing there, and Darby must have scrambled over the front seat and followed one of us through a door. When I asked if he was okay, I got a quiet, "Yes, Mistress," from the vicinity of my right elbow."

After I unlocked the back door, we all trouped into the shop. I hadn't even managed to lock the door behind me before Darby popped back into view and scurried to the center of the store, where he dropped to his knees, bowed his head, and said, "Your Majesty, forgive me I did not know I would be in your presence this day."

Your Majesty?

A small beam of light fell on Darby's bowed head, and flower petals rained down around him.

The little brownie raised his head. His expression was absolutely joyful. "Thank you, Your Majesty," he said. "I am very happy to see you as well."

He was talking to Myrtle.

"I'm afraid I do not understand," Beau said.

"Join the club," Tori said.

They both looked at me, as if I knew what the heck was going on.

"What?" I said. "Why am I supposed to be the one with all the answers?"

"*Hello?*" Tori said. "Resident witch?"

"Oh, right," I grumbled, "because I've *so* been knocking that one out of the ballpark tonight. Okay, Myrtle, what gives with the royalty thing?"

Darby inclined his head as if listening to someone, and then said, "Her Majesty has asked me to say to you, 'A girl is entitled to her secrets.'"

I rolled my eyes.

"Very funny, Myrtle," I said. Turning to Darby, I asked, "What is Myrtle, exactly?"

He looked at me like I'd grown a second head. "She Who Has Always Been," he said.

"Darby, *come on,*" I said. "Can I get a straight answer here, please?"

The brownie tilted his head to the side again and appeared to be concentrating. Then he said, "Her Majesty says that she is exactly who you have always known her to be, and I am to tell you that she has reconsidered the issue of the paint and is willing to look at the Cerulean Blue again."

Behind me I heard Tori say, "Yes!" I'm sure there was an accompanying fist pump, but I was too tired to turn around and verify that.

"Okay, fine, whatever," I said. "I'm too tired to deal with this right now. Myrtle, can you take care of Darby while we get some sleep?"

I was answered with the three-note trill Myrtle used to signal agreement.

Turning to Colonel Longworth, I said, "Will you be okay, Beau?"

His eyes were fixed on the Confederate Veterans Memorial across the street on the courthouse lawn. "If you are in agreement," he said, "I think I will spend some time there on the lawn thinking about my comrades in arms and perhaps take a stroll around the square."

"Okay, that's fine," I said. "We'll see you later."

As Tori and I started dragging ourselves upstairs, I looked back to see Darby apparently in rapt conversation with thin air. I was guessing he and Myrtle had a lot of catching up to do.

When I opened the door of the apartment, we were greeted by four fixed and steely feline gazes. The breakfast service was running almost two hours behind.

"I've got this," I told Tori, who was already headed for the couch.

She mumbled something that sounded like "thanks" before collapsing into the cushions. I fed the cats and stretched out on the bed, being careful to set the alarm on my phone. I swear I hadn't even closed my eyes before the dang thing went off. Tori was still snoring in the other room, so I took a quick shower before I woke her up.

"Hey," I said, shaking her shoulder lightly, "I'm heading downstairs."

"What time is it?" she mumbled.

"A little before 8:30," I said. "Mark and the guys will be here in half an hour and I need to open up."

"Okay. I'll be down in a few," she promised.

I left her sitting on the couch blinking in the morning sunlight that was streaming through the front windows. She looked like a disgruntled owl with partially magenta feathers.

Darby was waiting for me at the bottom of the stairs with a steaming cup of coffee in his hands. "Good morning, Mistress," he said. "I took the liberty of preparing a hot beverage for you."

Maybe Tori had a point about this house elf . . . excuse me, house *brownie*, concept.

"Darby, you are an angel," I said.

"No, Mistress, angels are. . . ."

I held up my hand to stop him.

"Don't tell me," I said. "I'm not awake enough for more metaphysical creatures right now."

That's when I took a sip of the coffee.

Oh. My. God.

How do you describe heaven in a cup?

Not only was the brew fragrant, strong and smooth, but it slid into my nervous system with quiet authority. I felt every cell in my body start to wake up.

"What did you put in this?" I asked.

Darby smiled. "It is to your liking?"

"Very much so," I said, "but I still want to know what you put in it."

"Nothing, Mistress," Darby said earnestly. "I found a selection of coffee beans in your storeroom. Rodney was quite gracious in explaining your daily routine to me."

Rodney explained my routine?

"You had a conversation with Rodney?" I interrupted.

"Of course," Darby said, blinking, "it would have been rude of me to ignore him."

Literal much?

"Fine. We'll sort that out later," I said. "Go on about the coffee."

"As I was saying, I found a selection of beans and merely mixed them to achieve the right blend," Darby said. "I also cleaned your coffee machine, calibrated the grinder, and adjusted the internal thermostat to reach the optimum level for brewing."

"What century did you say you're from?" I asked.

I meant it as a wisecrack, but again, literal.

"I was last in service in the 19th century, Mistress,"

Darby said helpfully.

"Okay, let me rephrase that," I said. "How did you know to do all that with the coffee and the machine?"

"Oh," he said, "Her Majesty introduced me to the Internet last evening."

Okay. Hold the phone. Myrtle was jacked in?

"She did, huh?"

"Yes," Darby said happily. "You now have a Facebook page showcasing the products in your store, as well as a Twitter feed and an Instagram account."

It was a good thing he gave me the cup of coffee first.

"Darby," I said, as patiently as I could, "I think you better show me what you've been up to."

When I followed the little guy into the storeroom, I was shocked to see Rodney sitting in front of my laptop peering at the screen.

"And just what do you think you're doing?" I asked, sitting down in the easy chair and peering over his shoulder.

Rodney pointed at the screen, which was displaying my new Facebook page—which already had 1,200 likes. The feed was full of photos of the renovations in progress, and a lot of upbeat posts about the new "coffee house."

I wasn't sure who did the typing—the rat, the brownie, or the store,—but they made for one heck of a social media team.

Fifteen minutes later, Tori was sitting beside me with her own cup of hot coffee, perfectly laced with half-and-half. Two sips in, she turned to me and asked, "Oh my God, what is in this? I feel like I've had 10 hours of sleep."

"Darby says he didn't do anything but blend the beans," I said. "Wait until you see what else he and Rodney have been up to."

She was staring open mouthed at the screen of the laptop.

"You did all this?" she asked Darby, who was so pleased with himself he was almost dancing in place.

"With assistance from Her Majesty and Rodney," he said graciously.

"Jinksy," she said, clicking a few keys, "we have better than 3000 followers on Twitter already. There are people on Facebook planning to come visit us when they drive the Parkway. And look at these pictures Myrtle put on Instagram. You have to let me keep working with these guys."

Raise your hand if you think I stood a chance of stopping them. Anybody? Anybody?

"Fine with me," I said. "There's your job, Darby. Help Tori make our coffee shop a success." I paused and then added, "And keep greeting me every day with a cup of this stuff."

Hey, I have to get some personal perks out of this situation.

"With pleasure, Mistress," Darby said happily.

When I left the room to go open the shop for the day, Rodney was sitting on Tori's shoulder, and she and Darby were deep in conversation about the wisdom of getting on Pinterest. We still had a cemetery full of ghosts to put back in their graves, but in general, things didn't seem to be getting worse.

Note to self. Never allow yourself to think that things aren't getting worse.

Halfway to the front door, Beau Longworth materialized in front of me. "Miss Jinx," he said, "I fear we have complications."

SEVEN

In case you don't know it, Southerners can have a real talent for understatement. The complication in question? Howard McAlpin.

During Colonel Longworth's exploration of the town square, he wandered into City Hall only to discover His Honor the Mayor attempting to reclaim the reins of power.

"He did *what*?!" I exclaimed as Beau described what he witnessed.

The Colonel patiently repeated himself. "In a fit of pique, Mr. McAlpin swept the current mayor's desk clean of its contents."

"And how did the mayor react?" I asked.

"Which mayor?" Beau asked.

"Beau," I said in exasperation, "the *living* one."

"Fortunately, the window of his office was open and he has allowed himself to believe that a rogue gust of wind was responsible," Longworth answered.

I looked across the street at the trees on the courthouse lawn. Not a leaf was stirring. The power of human beings to deny what is right in front of their eyes should never be underestimated.

"What were Howie and the councilmen doing when you left?" I asked.

Howie and the Councilmen. Now there's a band name for you.

"The deceased mayor appears to be particularly interested in the county land office," Beau said. "He was there when last I saw him."

Just then, Mark and his workers arrived. We said our good mornings, and my contractor brought up a sore subject with me. "Have you decided about the downstairs bathroom remodel?" he asked.

If we were going to open a coffee shop, we had to have public restroom facilities. The downstairs bathroom at the shop was in perfect working order, but the fixtures were old, noisy, and only dubiously up to code.

"Mark, seriously, not today," I said.

"Okay," he said, accurately reading my expression, "but you have to make a decision this week. If you wait for the inspector to give you the thumb's down, I'm already going to be on another job."

I promised to let him know by the next day and excused myself to go into the storeroom. After I filled Tori in on what Beau told me, I said, "I'm going over to City Hall and see if I can get Howie to knock it off. You're in charge."

"Take your bluetooth headset," Tori said.

Oh for God's sake.

"Tori, I am not going to have time to call you and give you a play by play," I said.

"I don't want a play by play," Tori said. "If you're wearing your headset and you start talking to yourself, nobody is going to think anything about it."

Oh.

"That's actually a really good idea," I admitted.

"I have them," Tori snarked.

As much as I hate to admit it, I went for an extremely adult response. I stuck my tongue out at her.

As Beau and I started across the street to the courthouse, he said, "May I ask what you are planning to do?"

Making a show of touching the headset in my ear, I said, "First, we need to find Mayor McAlpin."

"Do you have any legitimate business with the local government?" Beau asked.

"I could stop by Inspections and Permits and see if we're still set for them to take a look at Tori's apartment Friday," I suggested.

"While you are doing that," Beau said, "I will locate Mr. McAlpin."

Divide and conquer. I liked it.

The courthouse was an old, cavernous building with cool, echoing halls tiled in moss green. I passed the Sheriff's Office and waved to the dispatcher, repeating my greeting to the County Clerk. Even though I hadn't been in town long, I already knew everyone who worked in the courthouse and in the businesses that lined the square.

In the Office of Inspections and Permits, Sally Martin greeted me with her usual enthusiasm. "Why, Jinx Hamilton! Bless your heart, honey, how are you today?"

Yes, there are alternate meanings to the phrase "bless your heart." This was the good one.

"Hi, Sally," I said. "I'm good. How about you?"

"Oh, I'm just fit to be tied," she said, sighing heavily.

Here we go.

"Why's that?" I asked.

"M.J. is supposed to be mowing my grass today and danged if that man isn't off fishing again," she said.

Her husband, M.J., is the best fisherman in the county. He's famous in these parts for putting off an emergency appendectomy long enough to weigh in his catch at a bass tournament, and near *legendary* for his yearly trips to Oklahoma to compete in a noodling tournament.

Noodling involves catching catfish by getting in the

water with them and sticking your hand in the fish's mouth. I kid you not.

Anyway, I took a minute or two to commiserate with Sally. My Mom is a fishing widow, too, so I knew all the right things to say. At the appropriate juncture in the conversation, I asked about the scheduled inspection.

Sally looked at me funny and said, "Sugar, you could have called to ask me that question. Of course I'm gonna send Louie over. He'll be there first thing Friday morning."

Since I didn't want her to think I was questioning the efficiency of her office, I said, "Oh, I know I could have called. I just wanted an excuse to get out of the shop. Mark and the guys are working on the coffee shop today and all that hammering is driving me nuts."

That was an excuse no one would dispute, and Sally launched into her own story of enduring a home remodel the year before. Just then, I saw Colonel Longworth standing in the hallway trying to get my attention.

I had to stand there and listen to Sally long enough to make it sound like I cared, which involved making sympathetic noises and nodding a lot. Finally, she took a breath and I said, "Well, I guess I have to get on back to the store. I can't play hookie forever."

"Well, I do feel for you, sugar," Sally said. "You hang in there, now."

As I started for the door, something suddenly occurred to me. "Sally," I said, turning back toward her, "did you know a man named Howard McAlpin."

"Lord God in heaven," she said, "I sure did. What in the world made you ask about that jackass?"

I had another story ready that no one would disbelieve. "Oh, I was cleaning out more of Aunt Fiona's stuff and found an old campaign poster of his."

My aunt's approach to inventory can best be described

as "pack rat." Five years from now, I could still be telling people that I was "cleaning out her stuff" and they'd believe me.

"I don't doubt that," Sally said. "He used to wallpaper the town with those danged things every election. He died in office back in '83, and it was good riddance to bad rubbish if you ask me."

"Oh?" I said, innocently. "Why do you say that?"

"Well," Sally said, lowering her voice, "I hate to speak ill of the dead, but Howard's main reason for being mayor was to line his own crooked pockets. He was doing everything he could to drive the little stores in this town out of business. I'm really surprised that Fiona would have had one of his posters."

"Did I mention it was ripped in two?" I improvised.

Sally chuckled. "That sounds about right," she said.

"Why was he trying to shut the small shops down?" I asked.

"Rumor had it that he had a kickback deal with one of those big ole super stores like Wally World," she said. "You know how they just swallow up the local economy when they move in."

"So what happened?" I asked.

"Well, Howard was found dead at his desk," Sally said.

I was already not liking the sound of this.

"Heart attack?" I asked.

"Oh no," she said. "He had a swordfish bill stuck right through his heart."

Now let me tell you something. By virtue of the fact that I am a southerner, I am used to hearing strangely dichotomous statements come out of people's mouths, but that one got even me.

"He was murdered with a *fish*?" I said.

"That's what the official report says," Sally said, with a bemused smirk.

Now she had me hooked. Pun intended.

"Okay, I'll bite," I said. "What really happened?"

"He fell on a fishing trophy," she said, her eyes sparkling with barely suppressed mirth.

"The trophy was shaped like a swordfish?" I asked.

"Yep," she said. "A *brass* swordfish."

By this time, Beau had stepped into the office as well and was clearly as fascinated by this story as I was.

"Excuse me?" I said.

"Howard was into deep sea fishing," she said. "The trophy was a gaudy brass swordfish mounted on a marble base that sat on his desk for God and everybody to see. Dang thing weighed a ton. Howard tripped on the mat under his chair, fell on top of his desk, and ran that swordfish's bill straight into his heart. Bled out right there like a stuck pig."

"Seriously?" I asked, aghast at the mental picture her words painted in my mind.

"Yep," she said. "Damned idiot killed himself."

Beside me, Beau tapped his ear and pointed at my headset. He catches on quick.

"Oh, dang, Sally," I lied, "excuse me. I'm getting a call." I tapped the headset. "Hi . . . oh, I'm sorry, Tori . . . I'll be right back over. Hang on just a sec."

I looked at Sally and mouthed, "Sorry!"

She waved her hand in a shooing motion and said, "Go on, sugar. See you again real soon."

Still engaging in my fake conversation, I stepped out of the office with Beau. We walked a little ways down the hall. "Where is he?" I whispered.

"He and his associates are in an empty office on the second floor," the Colonel said. "They are quite frustrated by their inability to move objects in the physical world."

"But you told me McAlpin knocked everything off the current mayor's desk," I said. "How did he do that if he can't move objects?"

"That was an act of rage," Beau said. "The force of his anger accomplished that feat. His current goal is to examine records contained in file cabinets. That Mr. McAlpin cannot do, and he is quite annoyed."

"I'll bet," I said. "Okay. Show me."

Most of the functional offices of the Briar Hollow city and county government are contained on the first floor of the courthouse. The second floor harkens back to the days when the little town was more prosperous and in need of more political office space.

Beau's search tracked Mayor McAlpin and the spectral councilmen to a deserted corner office. When I turned the doorknob, my luck held. It was unlocked. Three mostly transparent heads swiveled when I stepped inside. The trio looked decidedly guilty until they recognized me.

"Oh," McAlpin said, "it's just you. What are you doing here?"

Minimize a girl, much?

"Yeah, it's me," I said, "and what the heck are *you* doing here?"

McAlpin's form rippled as if he was trying to stand up straighter. "I am an elected official," he said. "I *belong* here."

"You're a *dead* elected official, Howard," I pointed out. "You belong back . . ."

Back where? I had no intention of hazarding a guess about where politicians go when they die.

"Back wherever you've been since you killed yourself with a swordfish," I finished.

McAlpin's brow furrowed. "What are you babbling about, young woman?" he said. "I most certainly did not kill myself."

"Maybe not intentionally," I conceded, "but according to Sally Martin, you tripped at your desk and stabbed yourself in the heart with a swordfish trophy."

Both of the councilmen looked like they wanted to laugh, but didn't dare.

Howard bristled, sending an indignant ripple through his amorphous body. "Sally Martin doesn't have sense enough to pour . . ."

I stopped him mid-insult.

"Howard," I warned, "mind your manners."

McAlpin shot me a smirk. "Great," he said, "another thin-skinned woman with no sense of humor. Just what I need."

Great. Another egotistical narcissist. Just what I needed.

"Look," I said, "you can deny it all you want, but you were still found dead at your desk with a fishing trophy sticking out of your heart."

"That's ridiculous," he barked.

"I would tend to agree," I said sarcastically.

"I meant," he said, "that I kept that trophy pointed off to the side of my desk. There is no way I could have fallen forward and stabbed myself. I knew there was something suspicious about this whole death business. It was not in my five-year action plan. I must have been murdered."

Now tell me the truth, people. Does anybody put dying in their "five-year action plan?"

"Accidents happen, Howard," I said. "Death has a nasty habit of being a surprise."

"Not for me, it doesn't," he growled. "If I died like that, I was murdered, and I do not have the slightest intention of going anywhere until I find out who did it."

Not the answer I was looking for.

EIGHT

Issuing that ultimatum took every ounce of energy Howard had—literally. He stood in front of me flickering in and out like a dying fluorescent light bulb. For that matter, the councilmen weren't looking all that great either. The two men weren't impersonating strobe lights, but they were considerably fainter than when I'd entered the room.

"What's the meaning of this?" Howard demanded. The words came out like a static-filled radio broadcast.

"You have used all your available resources for the present," Beau explained, floating up beside me. "It will be a number of hours before your coherence reasserts itself."

"I don't see you blinking in and out," Howard crackled indignantly.

"Nor do you see me wasting my energy in useless tirades against the quite evident reality of my own demise," Beau observed mildly.

McAlpin glared at him, or at least he tried to glare. The effect was lost as his form grew more unstable. "Don't just stand there," he demanded, "plug me in or something."

The instant he said it, the image on a dying iPhone throwing a temper tantrum popped into my head. I couldn't keep from giggling, which only made McAlpin angrier.

"No can do, Howie," I said cheerfully. "See you later when your battery recharges."

Before he could reply, the late mayor blinked out entirely.

Turning to the Colonel, I asked, "How long before we have to deal with him again?"

"I do not image you will see His Honor the Mayor again until nightfall," Beau said, looking as relieved as I felt.

From across the room one of the councilmen cleared his throat. "Uh," he said tentatively, "what about us?"

"I hate to be the one to say it, guys, but you're fading fast," I pointed out.

"Where will we go?" the man asked fearfully.

That was a question for Beau, who picked the ball up right on cue.

"Do not concern yourself, sir," he said. "The sensation you will experience is very akin to being asleep. You will return later as well."

It didn't seem right to just leave and let the two men fade out alone since they were both clearly afraid, so I decided to get as much information out of them as I could while they were still visible.

"Do you gentlemen have names?" I asked.

"I'm Eldon," the first man said, "and he's Marty."

"Does your boss always behave like that?" I asked, gesturing toward the blank space where McAlpin had been standing.

"Pretty much," Eldon admitted. "By the way, you probably shouldn't call him Howie. That's what his mother called him and he doesn't like it."

So the Mayor had Mommy issues. Color me shocked.

"Noted," I said. "So what's your take on this murder theory of his? Did anybody dislike Howard enough to kill him?"

Marty laughed. "Pretty much everyone in town," he said.

Great.

"If everybody hated him," I said, "how did he get elected?"

The two men looked like I'd just tied them to straight chairs under the glare of a naked light bulb.

"For God's sake," I said, in exasperation, "you're already dead. What in the world do you think can happen to you if you tell me?"

"We'll have to listen to Howard for eternity," Eldon said instantly.

Okay. He had a point there.

I tried coming at my question from a different angle. "How long was Howard mayor?"

"Three-and-a-half terms," Marty said.

"The 'half' is because he died in office?" I asked.

"Oh," Marty said, frowning. "I forgot about that. I guess it was three and two halves."

How I kept a straight face when I asked the next question, I do not know. "So, Marty, what did you do as city councilman?"

"I was in charge of auditing the city's finances," he said proudly.

Before I could answer, both men were gone. Beau and I stood there a minute and then we both burst out laughing. The Colonel actually slapped his knee.

"I see that politicians have changed little since I was alive," he said, chuckling.

"Oh," I said, wiping my eyes, "we have much worse than Marty there. Let me tell you about this woman who was the governor of Alaska.

"Alaska is a state?" Beau said, his eyes widening. "I fear I am quite behind the times."

"You have a good excuse," I said, smiling.

We went back downstairs and exited the building. As I waited to cross the street, I said, "So when those guys pop back in, where will they be?"

"I can't say for certain," Beau admitted. "They may return to the cemetery or they could reappear in the courthouse."

"Well," I said, "at least we don't have to worry about Howard pulling any more stunts for a few hours. That's something. Are you going to hang around the store with us today?"

The question seemed to catch Beau off guard.

"Are you okay?" I asked with sudden concern. "You're not getting ready to blink out, too, are you?"

The old soldier regained his composure. "No," he said. "Even though I am far from my marker, I feel quite strong. It has just been a long time since I enjoyed freedom of movement or the engagement of a living companion. If I will not be underfoot, I think I would very much like to stay near you and Miss Tori today."

I might have other ghostly problems, but Colonel Longworth wasn't one of them. In my brief moment of panic, I realized I wanted the old man hovering—literally—in the background all the time. To use an old-fashioned word, the Colonel is stalwart. Until you've had a dose of that in your life, you may not get what I mean, but in the short time I'd known him, I had come to the instinctual understanding that Beau Longworth would always have my back.

"I'm glad you're here in town with us, Beau," I said, and I genuinely meant it.

The Colonel blinked a couple of times and then a slow smile spread over his face. "Young lady," he said, "that is the nicest thing anyone has said to me in more than a century. You see, although I do not like to dwell on it, there are aspects of being deceased that are, admittedly, rather lonely."

See? Understatement much?

We crossed the street and walked into my shop. I had to resist the urge to hold the door open long enough for Beau to pass. It's hard to get used to someone who can just serenely move straight through walls. To my surprise and pleasure, I spotted Chase McGregor standing in the back talking to my contractor.

Chase was wearing what I had come to regard as his work "uniform;" a long leather apron over a plaid shirt, softly worn jeans, and black boots he makes himself. He's not a big man, only standing about 6 feet, but he's broad chested and powerfully built. Add blue eyes and perpetually tousled dark hair to the picture and it makes for one heck of a view.

"Well, hello there," I said, going over to join them. "Don't you have a store to run?"

I blushed a little when Chase leaned down and gave me a light kiss, but it was a happy blush.

"Festus is manning the place for a few minutes," he said. "Mark called me over to show me what needs to get done this weekend."

Two explanations. Festus is Chase's lame ginger tomcat who spends most of his time in warm weather sprawled on the bench in front of the cobbler shop. In the winter, Festus switches to the bench just inside the front door in a direct line with the heating vent. He's a real innovator, that cat.

As for the weekend work, Chase helps Mark out from time to time with finishing details. Apparently over the next couple of days, I would have a handsome man in my shop installing the baseboards in Tori's apartment and helping to get her new furniture in place.

Out of the corner of my eye, I saw Colonel Longworth giving Chase the once over. "Is this your young man?" Beau asked, sounding very much like my father. Just to give you a visual on that reference, Dad was sitting at the kitchen table cleaning his shotguns the first time a boy came to pick me up.

Beau knew perfectly well that I was in no position to answer him at the moment, so he was free to continue his observations uninterrupted. "He's a comely fellow," the Colonel mused, "and gainfully employed, which certainly speaks in his favor. May I inquire as to his age, please?"

Doing my best to ignore my Confederate chaperone, I answered Chase. "Well, as long as Festus is in charge, all is well. What's the plan for the weekend work?"

Both men turned toward the construction in progress in the corner of the shop and launched into a discussion about the needed plumbing, which gave me a chance to mouth "stop it" to Beau.

The Colonel smiled at me beatifically. "I am merely looking out for your best interests, Miss Jinx," he said. "I assume that Mr. McGregor is from good people?"

Oh for God's sake. There it was. The Southern preoccupation with "your people."

"We will talk about this later," I hissed.

Mark and Chase both turned toward me with shocked expressions. "I thought you wanted to talk about it now," Chase said, looking confused.

"No," I said, flustered. "I mean . . . yes, I do . . . want to discuss it. I wasn't talking to you. Sorry, I was just . . . thinking out loud."

Chase gave me a strange look and then stared straight past me toward Colonel Longworth, furrowing his brow and squinting his eyes a little. "Is there smoke in here?" he asked.

Mark sniffed the air. "I don't smell anything burning," he said, sounding alarmed. "We haven't been doing any wiring today."

"It's just dust," I said quickly. "You guy's stirred up

about 40 years' worth when you moved those cabinets, and you have been cutting through the walls to put those pipes in."

Both men seemed to find my hurried explanations acceptable. They resumed their discussion. I caught Beau's eye, pointed to the storeroom and mouthed, "In there. Now!"

Still smiling, the Colonel said, "As you wish," and floated away completely unperturbed.

When Chase and Mark were finished talking, I went to the door with Chase. "I'm sorry I'm so scatterbrained today," I apologized. "I couldn't sleep last night. I guess I'm kind of out of it."

"That's okay," he said. "Everybody has an off day." He hesitated. "Have you done something different in here?"

It was my turn to frown. "Other than moving the cabinets, no. Why?"

Chase shook his head. "I don't know, something just seems different in the store. While I was talking to Mark I kept thinking I saw something out of the corner of my eye."

Uh-oh

"Like what?" I asked innocently.

"I'm not sure," he said, shaking his head. "Just my eyes playing tricks on me I guess."

Yeah, or a helpful brownie forgetting to do his invisibility cloak *thing*.

After Chase left, I went into the storeroom and found Colonel Longworth actually sitting in the armchair with his long, boot-encased legs crossed, chatting with Tori and Rodney, who was sitting on her shoulder.

"What was that whole *Father Knows Best* thing you were doing out there, Beau?" I demanded.

That was a total waste of a vintage TV reference.

"Fathers do know what is best for their daughters," he said, nonplussed.

"Whatever," I said, "but I'm kind of past grown."

"You are unmarried," he said, as if that explained everything.

Talk about Clash of the Centuries. I decided to just let it go, because frankly, the old guy *was* being kind of sweet, I just wasn't willing to admit that. I had another, more pressing question.

"What the heck happened out there anyway," I said. "Do you think Chase saw you?"

"Miss Tori and I were just discussing that very thing," Beau said. "She has a theory."

I plopped down beside Tori on the loveseat and reached up to scratch Rodney's nose as he scampered onto my shoulder.

"Let's hear it," I said.

After the day I was having, I didn't think anything could surprise me, but I have to hand it to my girl, Tori. She never disappoints.

NINE

"You think Myrtle is an *amplifier*?" I asked, frowning.

"Yeah," Tori said, drawing her legs up under her so she was sitting in something akin to the lotus pose. "I think Colonel Longworth is getting some extra juice from her or something. That's why Chase could kind of make out his outline."

"And how did you come to this conclusion?" I asked.

Without prompting, Beau leaned forward and gingerly picked a magazine up from the makeshift coffee table. Even though he was obviously out of practice manipulating objects, the copy of *People* was resting between the thumb and forefinger of his pale right hand.

Pale.

Not transparent.

For the first time since I'd met him in the cemetery, I couldn't see through Beau.

"Wow," I said. "That's a big change."

"An apt observation," Beau agreed mildly.

"I probably don't have to tell you this," I said to him, "but if Tori is right about this, you need to be careful where you stand."

Beau inclined his head in agreement. "We are ahead of your conclusions in that regard," he said. "The sunlight seems to have served to create something of a halo around

67

my form. I will keep to the shadows when others are present."

See what I mean? Fatherly inquisitions notwithstanding, Beau wasn't going to be a problem. In fact, by the time I get finished telling you this story, you'll see that he proved himself to be exactly the opposite.

"Did you tell Tori what happened at the courthouse?" I asked him.

"I was just recounting the financial abilities of Councilman Eldon when you came in," Beau grinned.

Tori let out a derisive snort. "Our tax dollars at work. *Not*."

My thoughts exactly. Given everything I'd learned over the past month, I'd come to the conclusion that sometimes you can cheat death a little, but taxes and inept politicians are pretty much here to stay.

"I'm not worried about the councilmen," I said, "but the star attraction of the undead political show is going to be a real pain in the backside until we can get him back where he belongs. I think it's time we learned more about the Honorable Howard McAlpin. For one thing, I want to know what Eldon meant when he said Howie served three-and-a-half terms."

"Two halves," Beau said in a droll voice.

I started to make a crack about "new math," but stopped myself. I couldn't even explain *that one* to the living.

Tori reached for her laptop and called up the website for *The Briar Hollow Banner*. I don't know who meticulously indexed the archives of the local small town rag, but all the issues from the 1800s forward are all online. Somebody at the *Banner* must have been very bored or very enamored of their brand new scanner to put in that much work.

With a few keystrokes, Tori found Howie's obituary. It was the usual exercise in post-mortem canonization. The writer more or less made the late mayor walk on water.

The language was so flowery, Howie might have even poured the water *in* the lake before taking a stroll on the surface.

"Go farther back," I suggested, "before Howie became the most popular corpse in town."

With a little more digging, we found out that Howard McAlpin became Briar Hollow's chief executive when his predecessor met an untimely demise involving a lawn mower, an excess of Miller Lite, and an electrical cord.

Hey, drunken yard work is much more hazardous than you might think—especially when done in your shorts, beer in hand, while the Christmas lights are still plugged in and glowing.

Once in office, Howie set out making enemies with a vengeance. From stringent leash ordinances in the land of hound dogs riding in the truck bed, to condemning properties to be auctioned by the city for profit, he attacked every sacred cow of small town life.

Oddly enough, however, with each election cycle, would-be opponents filed for the mayor's race only to drop out in a matter of days. By his third term, the one that ended with a swordfish to the heart, Howie ran for his office unopposed.

That fact didn't stop him from taking out full-page ads, however, touting a platform that called for bringing outside land developers into Briar Hollow to "eradicate the small-minded thinking of local business people who have kept our community stagnant for decades."

"Why do you suppose no one ran against him?" Tori asked, studying the screen.

"I would venture to say the Mayor had incriminating information on his would-be opponents," Beau suggested. "It is a standard political tactic."

I had to agree. Howie looked like a dirt digger if I ever saw one.

Just then Tori let out a low whistle.

"What?" I asked.

She turned the computer screen around so I could see a full-page, anti–Howie political ad paid for by Fiona Ryan. Among other things, Aunt Fiona had called the mayor "a dim-witted scoundrel with the political foresight of a thug for hire." No wonder Sally Martin had been surprised when I claimed to have found one of the guy's campaign posters in my aunt's store.

"I guess Eldon was right," I said. "There were plenty of people in this town who would have been happy to see Howie dead. But honestly, do we really care? All we need to do is get him back in his grave."

Tori shot me a "look" complete with cocked eyebrow. "Don't you mean all *you* have to do is get him back in his grave?"

My face flushed. There was no getting around the fact that I'd majorly screwed up last night at the cemetery. "I know, I know," I said a little miserably. "I blew it."

Tori's expression softened, but not much. "I don't suppose that same brilliant website you consulted in the first place has any suggestions about how to return spirits to their graves?"

As much as I hate to admit this, I had already checked Miss Elmira's Ethereal Emporium online for a possible solution. Nada. But she was having a sale on cauldrons.

Just then the bell on the front door jingled. I went out to discover that a tour bus had just deposited a group of retirees on the courthouse square. Even with the disruption of the workmen in the back corner, the unexpected crowd was a boon to my business. Several mentioned our new Facebook page and were disappointed that we weren't serving coffee yet. I handed out free essential oils samples, which seemed to satisfy them, and posed for several Instagram shots.

The customers kept us occupied all afternoon. It was well after 5 o'clock when I finally locked the front door and went back to the storeroom.

I didn't make it any farther than the door before I halted in my tracks. The makeshift coffee table was covered with a white linen cloth and a full dinner was laid out for us, complete with wine glasses and real silver flatware.

As soon as he saw me, Darby lifted the lid away from a domed platter to reveal a perfectly roasted chicken in a bed of rice and mixed vegetables.

"Darby," I said, my voice sounding a little breathless, "did you do all this?"

Smiling hopefully, the brownie said, "Yes, Mistress. I hope you are pleased. I also took the liberty of cleaning and organizing your kitchen this afternoon while you were occupied with business. Your feline companions are most interesting. Did you know Winston has an interest in classical literature?"

Huh.

That might explain why he comes running every time there's a Jane Austen movie on the TV . . .

Wait a minute.

My cat reads?

Okay. One earth-shattering revelation at a time. I own real silver flatware?

"Where did you find all this stuff?" I asked.

"In your living quarters, Mistress Jinx," Darby said, sounding a little uncertain. "Are you displeased?"

With the way that chicken smelled? Not a chance.

"No," I said, giving him a reassuring smile that caused his wizened little face to light up. "Not at all. This is *really* nice of you, Darby. I just didn't know I had all these things. You see, I've only been living here about a month."

I felt, more than heard, Tori come up behind me. "What

smells so good in here?" she asked, sounding like a hungry coonhound on the scent.

When I stepped aside, she let out a little gasp. "You *cook*, too?" she said to Darby.

The little man nodded. "I found some peculiar boxed items in the large ice chest in your kitchen," he said, "but they appear to belong to someone named Jenny Craig. I did not want to steal, so I prepared this instead."

Yeah. If Darby could cook like this, Jenny could dang well eat her own food from now on.

Tori and I sat down and watched in fascination as Darby poured our wine and expertly sliced the chicken. The food tasted as good as it looked. I turned to say something appreciative to our diminutive chef, but he was nowhere to be seen.

"Do you believe this?" I asked Tori.

Across from me, she chewed happily. "For food this good, I'll believe in unicorns." She paused for a second and then looked at me wide-eyed. "We haven't asked about unicorns," she said.

"Stop," I ordered firmly. "We have all the metaphysical creatures we can handle at the moment." Changing the subject, I asked, "Where's the Colonel?"

"When you were wrapping up the lavender soap for that woman in the loud green blouse, Beau told me he wants to be at the cemetery when the sun goes down," Tori answered, taking a sip of her wine. "He said he'll reconnoiter the situation and be back here 'as soon as practicable.'"

We both laughed. "He's a sweet old guy," I said, "and that's what has me worried."

Tori frowned. "Worried how?"

Even with the steady stream of customers, I'd had plenty of time to think throughout the afternoon. "Well," I said, "I guess we can agree that I didn't know what I was doing when I raised a whole cemetery of ghosts."

"No argument from me," Tori said. "So?"

"So," I said, "that means I not only have no idea how to put the new ghosts back, I don't know what will happen to the old ones when I try."

Tori's face fell. "Oh. My. God," she said. "You're afraid you'll make all of them go away, aren't you?"

I nodded. For as much as I had wanted to set the spirits free from their confinement in the graveyard, I hadn't planned to banish them or anything. I mean, I didn't want to hold them back from whatever might be . . . *next* . . . or did I?

They were our friends now. I couldn't imagine not watching Jeff hang on every word Tori read to him from *Sports Illustrated* or listening to Miss Lou Ella try to talk me into ratting my hair up into a bouffant.

And then there was Beau. He'd only been here at the store with us for one day and I already loved having him around.

Tori set her mouth in a firm line. "Jinksy," she said, "no more wonky web magic. You can't do *anything* until you really know what you're doing."

"Agreed," I said, "but what are we going to do with this herd of ghosts I've let loose?"

Spearing a potato with her fork, Tori said, "Oh, come on! How much trouble could a few extra ghosts cause? We can manage it."

Famous last words.

TEN

Tori and I had been enjoying our catered supper so much, neither one of us noticed when the sun went down. It wasn't until I heard a polite cough from the doorway that I looked up to realize the front of the store was dark. Beau Longworth stood just inside the room. The look on his face told me instantly we were in for trouble.

"I tried," he said simply, his voice filled with regret.

Uh-oh. That did *not* sound good.

"Tried what?" I asked, not really wanting to hear the answer.

"To get them all to stay in the cemetery," the Colonel answered. "I'm afraid they chose not to listen."

Tori and I both got up without a word and followed his faintly glowing form to the big front windows. The entire courthouse square was filled with wandering spirits. I watched with both fascination and pity as an elderly man stood in front of an empty storefront that had apparently been his business in life. He was rummaging through his pockets, I assumed searching for his keys. Suddenly it dawned on him that he could walk through the door, but when he did, his pale, luminescent form darted frantically back and forth across the darkened windows.

Even half a block away, we heard his voice raised in

alarm. "Help!" he cried. "Someone call the police. I've been robbed!"

A few sympathetic spirits milled toward him murmuring support, but my attention was drawn to a spectral police officer in full uniform. He was standing in the middle of the intersection to our left, which was now regulated by a traffic light. Oblivious to this fact, he blew forcefully on his whistle, gesturing for an oncoming car to stop only to have a Honda Civic run right through him.

The officer looked down at his body in horror, glancing around frantically. "Stop that car!" he yelled, blowing on his whistle again. "That jerk just tried to run me down."

We watched at least a dozen of these incomprehending melodramas play out around the square. Beside me Tori said, in a choked voice, "Jinsky, this is awful. We have to do something to help them."

His own voice thick with emotion, Beau said, "I tried to explain to them that they are no longer part of the world of the living. They did not believe me. Every one of them thinks they are neglecting the details of their lives."

Even though it was an incredibly personal question, I had to ask. "Was it like this for you at first, Beau?"

The old soldier shook his head. "Not exactly," he said. "I was a cavalry officer. My men were escorting wagons of supplies when we were ambushed a few miles outside of town. We charged the attacking Union forces and I took a Minie ball in the chest. I remember the sensation of falling off my horse and striking the ground."

He paused and swallowed hard. "I was grateful that Sampson, my mount, was uninjured in the fray," Beau said. "He was a faithful companion to me for many years. I watched him nuzzling my fallen body and knew that I had been killed. Poor Sampson, he was far too upset for any other possibility to be the truth."

Dear God. All these years later, the Colonel was more

upset about his horse than his own death. I never wanted to hug someone so bad in my life.

Beau cleared his throat and continued with his story. "In those days it was not practical to transport bodies over long distances," he explained. "I have come to understand that in modern times there are methods of preservation, but we were buried here, in the local cemetery a day or so later."

"Were you born around here, sir?" I asked. Suddenly, I really hoped there had been mourners when this gallant gentleman was laid in his grave.

"I am a native son of Tennessee," he said proudly. "After the war, my wife and daughter came to Briar Hollow to visit my grave. They are responsible for the obelisk that now marks my resting place."

Well, that was something. "Why didn't they take your . . . remains . . . home?" I ventured.

He turned to look at me, smiling sadly. "Almira, my wife, knew me well," he said. "My place was here, with my men."

Frowning, I said, "But, Beau, you're the only Civil War soldier I've seen at the cemetery."

"My boys rest in peace," he said simply. "I do not."

Before I thought, I asked, "Why not?"

Colonel Longworth inclined his head slightly, but then raised his eyes. "Because they were killed under my command," he said, as if he were admitting to having committed a heinous crime. "I was not vigilant that day. I chose a road for our transit without proper reconnaissance. My men died because of my foolish impatience."

There was nothing to say to that.

When I first met Beau, he explained that my Aunt Fiona, who visited the cemetery regularly, believed the spirits there had unfinished business. He didn't bother to add that the business that kept him walking the earth could never be finished.

We silently turned our attention back to the milling crowd of ghosts in the square. A trio of middle-aged housewives, circa 1950-something, walked past the window, and I heard one of them say, "Let's see if Aggie has any good sales today. I need a new dress to wear to Leona's for bridge Thursday night." They were on their way to the dress shop two doors down.

So far none of the spirits seemed to be doing anything threatening or that would call attention to themselves—other than the problematic Howard McAlpin, and so far he was nowhere to be seen.

Those were all positives. And after all, we were the only ones who could see the ghosts . . . weren't we?

I put the question to Beau. I didn't like his answer.

"You and Miss Tori are the only living souls who can see these spirits for now," he said. "But, like Mayor McAlpin yesterday, as they are thwarted in their attempts to resume their normal lives, and the more they are ignored by the living, their frustration will grow, and with it, their anger. I would anticipate that there will be . . . incidents."

Great. Just freaking great.

"So what do we do?" Tori asked.

Before either of us could answer her, I heard a gasp somewhere near the vicinity of my elbow and looked down to see Darby standing beside me. Well, okay, more like cowering behind me.

"Darby," I said, "what is it? Are you okay?"

The little man looked up at me with round, frightened eyes. He was trembling.

"She is here, Mistress, " he whispered.

I don't know about you, but I had more than reached my quota of prophetic statements for one evening. Couldn't anybody just deliver the bad news and get it over with?

Resigning myself to the next layer of complication headed our way, I asked the inevitable question. "'She' who?"

Darby shook his head vehemently and took a step back. "Please, Mistress," he pleaded. "Do not make me say her name. She will find me."

Great. We had a Lady Voldemort on our hands. She Who Will Not Be Named.

But I didn't say that or anything else snarky. Darby was too scared for me to be impatient with him.

"It's okay," I said soothingly. "Just point at her."

Now shaking violently, Darby raised one hand and extended his index finger toward the courthouse. "There," he said, in a voice so soft I had to bend down to hear him. "She stands in the shadow of the gray soldier."

I followed his gaze toward the granite Confederate Veteran's monument on the courthouse lawn. At the base of the statue, a lone woman stood perfectly still watching the bedlam around her with an expression I can only describe as bemused.

She was tall and lean with sharp, hawkish features. A long mane of red hair tumbled around her shoulders, blending into the folds of the flowing black cloak that covered her body and pooled on the ground around her feet.

As I studied her, the woman seemed to become aware of my gaze. Her eyes lifted toward the store and met my own.

She smiled.

Crap.

ELEVEN

Nobody argued when I suggested we step away from the window. The red-haired woman continued to stare toward the store with that creepy smile on her face as we retreated into the shadows. Even when I knew we were hidden from her view, I had the uneasy sensation that she was still watching our every move.

Darby was so frightened by this time, he was letting out snuffling whimpers. Rather than tower over his diminutive frame and talk down to him, I knelt on the floor and put my hands on his arms.

"Darby," I said, waiting to continue until he was looking right at me. "I'm not going to let anyone hurt you. Do you understand?"

The brownie nodded, but the eyes that looked out at me from his wizened features were still huge with fright.

He wasn't going to like what I had to say next, but I really didn't have a choice. "I need you to tell me about that woman . . ." I began.

The words were barely out of my mouth before Darby started shaking his head and began trying to pull away from me. That's when Myrtle intervened. The air around me warmed just slightly, creating a slight humming sensation on my skin. A faint blue light bathed us in its glow. I heard a sound like a mother humming a lullaby to a fussy baby. I wasn't anywhere near as scared as Darby, but it made *me* feel better, too.

The brownie turned his eyes upward, and I knew he was listening to Myrtle. Gradually the terror in his eyes receded to something more akin to the worst anxiety attack on record. I knew he was still horribly uncomfortable, but whatever Myrtle had said to him, the little man found his voice again.

"Mistress Jinx," he said, "the woman by the stone soldier is the sorceress, Brenna Sinclair. She followed Master Alexander to this land, and she is the reason Mistress Knasgowa was bound to her grave."

I hate to be redundant, but double crap.

Darby's statement hung in the air until Beau cleared his throat. "Perhaps we should adjourn to the storeroom," he suggested. "This would appear to have the makings of a lengthy tale."

What did I tell you about the Southern talent for understatement?

"That's probably a good idea," I agreed, "but what do we do about What's-Her-Name out there on the square?"

Tori took a cautious step or two toward the window. After scanning the scene, she said, "I don't see her anymore, Jinksy. I think she's gone."

"Is that good or bad?" I asked the group in general.

Darby was the one to answer. "If the sorceress had business with you on this night, Mistress, you would know it already."

Ominous, much?

We all filed into the storeroom, where Rodney was waiting for us, pacing back and forth on the shelf in front of his condo. Even the rat's spidey sense was firing at full strength. I held out my hand and let him scamper up my arm. He crawled inside the collar of my shirt and wrapped himself around my neck.

"Okay, Darby," I said, settling down in the easy chair, "tell your story."

Beau was right. The tale was a real whopper. Let me give you the highlights.

In the 17th century in Scotland, a group known as the Covenanters got majorly ticked off when the Stuart monarchs insisted on sticking by the whole Divine Right of the Monarch *thing*. If you're light on your European history, the short version is that the kings believed they ruled at the will of God. That meant the king was also the head of the Presbyterian Church of Scotland.

As a Southern Baptist, I can tell you that we regard modern Presbyterians as one of those oddly dignified denominations that couldn't let out with a proper "amen" to save their lives. You're not going to find any raised-hand-swaying parishioners in that crowd. Now, they're not as downright, unfathomably strange as the Episcopalians, but danged close. A few centuries ago, however, at least in Scotland, the Presbyterians apparently had a whole lot more spunk.

The Covenanters insisted that only Jesus Christ himself could be the head of the Church, and they were willing to fight in defense of that position. In 1679, their forces were defeated at the Battle of Bothwell Brig. The prisoners were carted off to Edinburgh and put on public display. Most of them caved and swore loyalty to the Stuarts, but about 250 hardcore Covenanters refused to budge.

The King decided to send them off to the New World as slaves to punish their hardheadedness. The prisoners were put on a ship called the *Crown of London*, but it ran aground in the Orkney Islands on December 10, 1679, off a place called Scarvataing. According to Darby, one crewman managed to survive, but it was believed that everyone else went down with the ship. Bodies washed up for weeks. They were all dead, or so the islanders thought.

The morning after the ship was driven onto the rocks, when the sky was still dark with scudding storm clouds, a local woman, Brenna Sinclair, found a survivor named Hamish Crawford. He was barely alive, and Brenna knew if she reported her discovery, he'd be imprisoned again.

Instead, Brenna took Hamish into her home, a solitary house high on a cliff overlooking the ocean. There, she nursed him and the two fell in love. As Darby related the tale, no one in the area could quite remember when Brenna started living in the house. No one knew if she'd ever had a husband, and even more oddly, no one questioned the fact that she was a woman making her way alone in the world.

At that time, neither the islanders nor Hamish Crawford knew that Brenna Sinclair was a sorceress, already hundreds of years old. Long before anyone cared about who was running the Presbyterian Church, Brenna forged a pact with the dark side that won her the biggest sweepstakes prize of them all—immortality.

If you've ever seen the *Highlander* movies, you already know that immortality is not without its complications. When you can't die, you have to *pretend* to croak every 75 years or so, re-creating yourself with a new identity so you won't get caught.

In the 17th century, that was a lot easier. You just picked up and moved far enough away that nobody from your old neighborhood would ever come around and run into you by accident, which is what Brenna Sinclair did when she moved to the Orkney Islands.

In the course of a few months after she rescued Hamish Crawford, two things happened: Brenna came up preggers and Hamish found out he'd been sleeping with a witch. That put the couple at cross-purposes for more than one reason. Brenna, who believed that she had sacrificed all traces of her humanity in exchange for eternal life, did not know she could conceive a child.

As she sat with her hand resting on her swelling belly, Brenna dreamed of the powerful line of magical descendants she would cultivate from the new bloodline growing in her body. She said nothing to the man who slept uneasily by her side each night, but Brenna had no intention of ever letting Hamish Crawford go. If he could impregnate her once, he could do it again.

For his part, Hamish lay night after night staring into the darkness, tormented by the thought that his seed had been used to spawn a child of the devil. The devout Christian in him wanted to see the baby and its mother burned for the abominations they were, but his heart was torn. How could he be party to murdering an innocent child who had not asked to be conceived?

In his torment, Hamish reached out to Duncan Skea, scion of an ancient Orkney family said to quietly keep to the old beliefs that had guided the island people in the days before the coming of Christianity. Duncan listened sympathetically to Crawford's tale and advised him to play along until the child was born. Together they hatched a plan to drug Brenna, imprison her, and kidnap the infant.

I'll say one thing for Duncan Skea and Hamish Crawford. They had guts. It's pretty hard to hide on an island. The Orkneys are actually an archipelago, a group of islands, that altogether cover about 382 square miles. But even with that expanded space, Hamish never would have escaped from Brenna without Duncan's help.

On the night of his son's birth, Hamish wiped Brenna's sweating brow and, gazing down at the baby in her arms, and offered the exhausted woman a drink of cool water. Brenna frowned at the taste, but it was already too late. The potion was in her system and she fell into a deep sleep.

Quickly summoning Duncan, the two men carried Brenna to a secluded cave and placed her inside. As Hamish watched, Duncan spoke quiet words over the entrance, which closed up before his wondering eyes, forming a solid wall of rock. Leaving his son in Duncan's care, Hamish headed back to mainland Scotland and exited the story altogether.

If you haven't put it together already, Duncan was Alexander Skea's great-grandfather by an act of child abduction. One-hundred-and-seven years later, the Scotsman who came to the New World and ultimately settled in Briar Hollow, North Carolina was the direct descendant of Hamish Crawford and the sorceress, Brenna Sinclair.

That night in 1679, Duncan named the crying baby boy Alistair. Before Hamish Crawford slipped into a boat and disappeared into the night, Duncan promised to raise the child as his own, training him to use his powers for good. In time, Alistair grew to manhood and sired a son, Angus, who in turn fathered Alexander, born in 1766.

Everything had been working out great up to that point. In each generation, Brenna's blood grew more diluted, and the Skeas became less concerned that they had brought black magic into their family line. Alistair and Angus were good men, well-respected in their communities, who quietly observed the old traditions without calling attention to themselves. Alexander showed every sign of following in their footsteps, that is until Brenna finally managed to escape.

Darby didn't know all the details, only that Angus Skea burst into his son's bedroom before dawn one morning in 1786 and told Alexander he must leave immediately for the New World. At 20 years of age, Alexander knew the truth about his origins and did not argue with his father.

Taking Darby with him, the young man boarded a ship for America. As Alexander looked back at the receding coastline of the Orkneys, he saw a red-haired woman standing on the shore. She raised her hand in a gesture of farewell, and the light, salty breeze that blew over the waters carried her whispered words straight to the ear of her great-grandson. "Run if you will, Alexander Skea, but I will find you."

It took his vessel three months to reach the coast of the Americas, a time when fearful nightmares disrupted Alexander's restless slumber just as feverish vigilance colored his days. Darby spoke of how his master stood on deck scanning the horizon, half expecting to see red-haired Brenna astride a sea serpent rise from the waters of the Atlantic to pull him down into the bottomless depths.

As soon as Alexander and Darby disembarked, they headed off for the remote frontier with the intent of never being seen again. But in North Carolina, Alexander's plans changed the moment he first looked into the black eyes of a Cherokee woman named Knasgowa. Overcome by her beauty, Alexander could not bring himself to move on. Finally, in a torment of love and terror, he told Knasgowa the entire story, only to learn that she, herself, was a witch.

"My Mistress was more than powerful enough to protect Master Alexander and myself," Darby said, love and admiration coloring his tones. "We were safe all the long years of her life, until in her 83rd year, my Mistress fell ill with cancerous growths that caused her to grow thin and weak. That is when she could no longer hide my Master and the sorceress Brenna Sinclair came to Briar Hollow."

With the last of her strength, Knasgowa taught Alexander how to bind Brenna to her own spirit for eternity. "My Master did not want to work the magic," Darby said. "He could not bear to think of his wife locked in a dark struggle for all time with an evil sorceress, but nor could he stand the idea that his own blood would be used for Brenna's plans to create a dark dynasty."

When Knasgowa was near death, she had Alexander carry her to the cemetery. There, they waited for Brenna. When she appeared, Knasgowa, though thin and frail, held the sorceress at bay as Alexander, tears streaming down his face, recited the words of the binding spell.

Darby's small body shook as he described what happened next. "Brenna's screams tore at the night," he said, "but my Mistress held fast to her with her dying breath. Together they were sucked into the earth, which closed over them. The blackness that obscured the moon rolled away and the stars once again shone in the sky. Master Alexander, wracked with grief, bade me stay with my Mistress, guarding her tomb for all time lest any evil servant of Brenna Sinclair's sought to free her from her prison."

With that, the little man looked at me, clearly finished with his story. There seemed to be only one question to ask.

"Darby," I said, "why didn't you stop me when I started reciting that spell over Knasgowa's grave?"

The brownie blinked as if I'd just asked something very foolish. "My Master charged me to guard his wife from evil, Mistress Jinx," he said. "You are not evil."

I can't tell you why, but that brought tears to my eyes. What I had done was a foolish accident, but my intention had been pure. Little did I know that I was about to open a sort of hell gate, one that Brenna Sinclair walked right through and into the 21st century.

At that moment, looking down at Darby's earnest little face, I have to admit I wished I was a little bit evil. Something told me that fooling Brenna the third time wasn't going to be any walk in the park.

Brother, was I ever right.

TWELVE

After Darby finished talking, we all just sat there, stunned. What can you say to a story like that? My mind reeled. Two days before, talking Tori out of a $10,000 coffee pot was my biggest problem. Now I had a ghost hollering murder, a courthouse square full of restless spirits, and a pissed off immortal sorceress.

I must have looked as overwhelmed as I felt because Tori rested her hand on my knee to get my attention. When my eyes focused on her, she said in a tone that didn't invite discussion, "You need to get some sleep."

Huh? It couldn't be more than . . . I glanced at the clock. A quarter of one. How the heck did that happen?

Before I could protest that we didn't have time for sleep, Beau cut in.

"Miss Tori is correct," he said. "None of the wandering souls out there are yet cohesive enough to cause a disruption in the physical world. There is no more that can be done tonight. You should take some time to come to terms with this new information. You will not make good decisions if you are exhausted."

My nerves were so shot, their kindness brought sudden tears to my eyes. I looked up into Beau's pale face and asked tremulously, "You'll stand watch?"

The old soldier drew himself up as if preparing for battle. He reached to lay a hand on my shoulder, and I actually felt the cool pressure of his fingers.

"Have no fear in that regard," he told me gently. "I will stand watch in the night."

Little Darby moved up next to my spectral friend and echoed his words, "I, too, will stand watch in the night, Mistress."

That did me in. Hot tears rolled down my cheeks.

Even if the two of them did make about as ridiculous a pair as Danny DeVito and Arnold Schwarzenegger in *Twins*, I knew Beau and Darby would both fight a circle saw for me.

No, I don't know why we say that in the South, but just go with the visual. Hand-to-hand combat with a power tool pretty much screams "loyal."

I gave in and agreed to call it a night.

Tori had to help me disentangle Rodney from around my neck. The little rat was sound asleep, but when I put him in his nest box, he opened one eye and let out a worried squeak.

"It's okay," I whispered. "Beau and Darby are on the case. I'll see you tomorrow. Sweet, cheesy dreams, little buddy."

Rodney nodded his head and was instantly out for the count, but I still had to pry his tiny protective paw off my index finger.

As soon as Tori and I made it through the door of my upstairs apartment, I dropped down on the rug and started scooping up cats. I needed all the feline comfort I could get. Winston buried his face in my collar, which made me giggle. His whiskers tickled.

"You like my new perfume?" I asked, scratching his ears. "It's called *Eau d' Ro Dent.*"

Tori disappeared into the kitchen, giving me a few minutes alone with the guys. Maybe you have to be a crazy cat lady to understand, but sometimes nothing sets the world right like the sound of purring and the feel of warm fur.

By the time she reappeared a few minutes later, I was starting to feel better. Still, I gratefully accepted the steaming mug of chamomile tea she held out to me with an encouraging smile.

"Thanks, Mom," I said, cradling the cup in my hands.

That won me a set of rolled eyes. "Your mom never made chamomile tea for you in her life," she said.

True. Kelly was more the "knock the kid out with NyQuil" type mom. Which actually might have been the better choice right at that moment considering how wired I felt.

Extricating myself from Winston's embrace, I carried my tea into the bedroom and sipped at it while I got ready for bed. It was a little sweeter than I would have made it, but the warmth felt comforting, so I drank it anyway.

Out in the living room, I could hear Tori making up the couch, talking to the cats as they "helped." All four felines were Olympic-quality athletes at Freestyle Hand Under the Blanket.

We both turned our lights off at the same time, which was just a cue for the conversation to begin. Some talks are better negotiated under the cover of darkness.

"Tori," I said, my voice sounding small even to my own ears, "what have I done?"

A sigh came from the living room. "I knew you were blaming yourself," she said. "You gotta knock that off."

"Exactly who else is there to blame?" I asked.

"Oh, I don't know," she said, "maybe Fiona for giving you the magic. Or Alexander Skea for turning tail and running to the New World. And then there's this Brenna bitch for wanting to live forever. 'Cause, really, narcissistic much?" She paused and then added brightly, "Oh, I know.

We can put it all on Howie and the Councilmen, or, as they're better known, The Ungrateful Dead."

In spite of the fact that I was awash in equal parts guilt and good, old-fashioned fear, I laughed. The iron bands around my chest loosened up a little bit and I felt like I could breathe again. That's what a BFF is supposed to do for you. Tori has the skill nailed. She can always make me laugh when I need it the most, and she helps me find my courage every time.

"That sounds better," she said approvingly. "You can't blame yourself, Jinksy. All this stuff was set in motion long ago . . ."

"In a galaxy far, far away," I interrupted. "So how about we just blow up the Death Star and go play with Ewoks?"

Seriously, if the Force is strong with you, *Star Wars* will give you all the answers.

"Works for me," Tori agreed, "but as much as I hate to point this out, you're Luke Skywalker in this story."

Which sucked Wookie . . .

You get the picture.

If I was Luke, then we were at least a galaxy shy of anything that passed for an answer because my Obi Wan Kenobi was nowhere to be seen.

———

"Fiona," Amity Prescott said, turning away from the front windows of her shop, "we're asking too much of Jinx."

At the back of the store, Fiona Ryan's spirit glowed in the dim light. "We have no choice, Amity," she said. "Brenna has been set free. Jinx is our only hope now."

Amity said nothing for a minute, watching as the ghost of Lemuel Maddox pushed a spectral broom outside the empty building that had once been his hardware store.

"It's disconcerting to know so many of them," she said

finally, gesturing toward the pale shades of her former friends and neighbors milling around the dark courthouse square.

"We both grew up here," Fiona said, floating up to stand beside her. "Of course we're going to know them."

"I cannot believe Jasper McCain buried Martha in that dress," Amity said absently. "Look how big her butt looks in that thing."

Fiona smiled. "Well, to be fair to Jasper, Martha was laying down in the casket. We couldn't see her butt."

"It's the principle of the thing," Amity said stubbornly. "Just because a woman is dead doesn't mean she shouldn't look her best. I mean for God's sake, what about that pink polyester monstrosity your little sister laid you out wearing? Did you own that damn thing or did Kelly actually pay money for it?"

Fiona scoffed. "Land of Goshen no, I didn't own it," she said. "If ever a fabric was the tool of the devil it's polyester. That whole getup was Kelly Ann's idea, and it was on her dime, not mine."

Still frowning, Amity said, "Your little sister could help her daughter with all of this if she just would. She's mule stubborn about her magical heritage."

Sighing, Fiona said, "Let's sit down. My feet hurt."

"Fiona," Amity said, "you're dead. Your feet can't hurt."

"Fine," Fiona countered, "but if I were alive they would be hurting. And besides, we can't do anything at the moment but stand here and watch, which I, for one, don't want to do."

Still grumbling a little under her breath, Amity followed Fiona's spirit back to the sitting area she'd arranged next to the cash register. In addition to selling art and pottery, Amity taught 'Draw Pictures While Drinking Wine' classes once a week. By the time she uncorked the third bottle, some of her patrons needed a soft place to rest their creativity.

"If we still had a proper coven, we could handle this whole fiasco in half an hour," Amity said, plopping down on the floral loveseat. "Brenna Sinclair wouldn't have a chance."

"That's a bit optimistic even for you, Amity," Fiona said, taking one of the chairs. "You've stood by Knasgowa's grave the same as I have and you've felt the power. We were raised on the legend of what happened the night their souls were bound for eternity."

"Which is why you should have prepared Jinx with proper lessons in witchcraft!" Amity said, annoyance and frustration punctuating her words. "Seriously, Fiona, what were you thinking? You just handed that poor child her powers without a whit of preparation. Is it any wonder she's making mistakes right and left?"

Fiona's eyes flashed defensively. "You talk like I planned all this, Amity," she said, sounding wounded. "I had absolutely no idea Jinx would ask for me to awaken her magic. Thanks to my pious little sister turning her back on our lineage, I didn't even think Jinx knew about our magic."

"Are you so sure she did?" Amity asked. "It sounds to me like the girl made a sleepy, off-hand remark and you jumped on it."

Fiona opened her mouth to protest, then shut it and fell silent.

"I'm right, aren't I?" Amity pressed.

"You're half right," Fiona said. "Jinx did ask for magic, but, no, she didn't know what she was doing. I just couldn't let the power die with me, Amity. Jinx is the last of our line and her potential is enormous."

Amity shook her head. "I understand that," she said, "and I probably would have done the same thing, but why aren't you helping her more now? Why didn't you tell her about Knasgowa's grave?"

"Because she wasn't ready," Fiona said. "I wanted her to get comfortable with her powers first. It never occurred to me she'd go raise a cemetery full of spirits."

"And do we know exactly *why* she did that?" Amity asked pointedly.

"Because she felt sorry for the souls trapped at the graveyard," Fiona said, her voice filled with loving pride. "She did it because she has a good heart."

Setting her mouth in a firm line, Amity said, "That good heart is not going to help with Brenna. And just how do you think Jinx is going to feel when she finds out the truth about Chase McGregor?"

"I think we have more than enough problems right now, Amity Prescott, without letting that particular cat out of the bag," Fiona said briskly.

Amity cocked an eyebrow in her direction. "*Cat* being the operative term," she said sardonically.

"That will be more than enough out of you," Fiona said. "I have every intention of talking to Jinx tomorrow. I would have materialized tonight, but Tori and Colonel Longworth were right; Jinx was exhausted. She needed some sleep. Besides, Myrtle will never let Brenna come into the shop."

"Well, thank heavens for that," Amity said, "but I wish you'd let me tell Jinx the truth about myself."

"No," Fiona said. "If you uncloak your powers, Brenna will sense you. We have to wait."

"For what, exactly?" Amity asked.

Fiona smiled. "For Jinx to fully embrace her powers," she said. "Then she'll know that she's more than a match for any black witch who crosses her path, including Brenna Sinclair."

"If she lives that long," Amity muttered darkly.

THIRTEEN

Whether it was the effect of the tea or just exhaustion, I did sleep that night. I woke up to the sound of Tori feeding the cats in the kitchen, which allowed me the luxury of a few more minutes under the covers. I was staring at the ceiling thinking when Tori said from the doorway, "Knock, knock."

I raised my head and saw that she was holding a cup of coffee in each hand. "Oh my God," I said, "the Angel of Caffeination. Good morning."

Tori laughed and walked to the edge of the bed to hand me one of the cups. I scooted up against the headboard, making room for her to sit down at the same time.

"How did you sleep?" she asked.

"Amazingly well," I said. "I never believed that chamomile worked, but it sure did last night."

"Well, duh." Tori grinned. "Of course it worked. I spiked it with cherry vanilla Nyquil."

I rolled my eyes. "God, you *are* turning into my mother."

"On the matter of Nyquil knockout drops, Kelly has a point," Tori said. "Seriously, you needed some sleep, and you were all set to lay in here and worry all night."

Taking a sip of my coffee, which was fragrant and bold (see? the whole barista thing is contagious), I said, "Don't you think we kind of have a few things worth worrying about?"

"Yeah," she conceded, "but I could see in your eyes that you were making up stuff to add to the worry pile. Come on, Jinksy, I know you. You are totally a worst case scenario kind of gal."

I looked down into my cup, absently running my index finger around the rim. "We've got a good thing started here," I said softly.

Tori shifted on the bed. "Go on," she prompted.

Before I could lose my courage I blurted out, "I don't want Chase to find out about all this and think I'm nuts and never want to have anything to do with me ever again."

And immediately felt like a total idiot.

"I thought that might be part of it," Tori said, completely ignoring my embarrassment. "You really like this guy, don't you?"

Still looking down at my cup, I nodded, but didn't say anything.

"Well, I do get why you're worried," she said in an exaggerated, sympathetic tone. "I mean, it's not like you've had great luck in the boyfriend department."

My head snapped up. "What the heck is that supposed to mean?" I asked, instantly indignant.

Tori regarded me with a cocked eyebrow. "Really, Jinksy? Do I need to list them off?"

Busted.

"You're not a heck of a lot better," I grumbled.

"Agreed," she said, "which is why I think Chase McGregor is a real catch. I mean, honestly, he's as crazy about cats as you are. You will *never* find another guy with that particular qualification."

Returning my gaze to the surface of my coffee, I said, "I don't want to screw any of this up. Not the store. Not the magic. And not Chase."

Tori reached out and caught my free hand, squeezing my fingers. "You won't," she said simply.

"How do you know?" I asked uncertainly.

"Because I won't let you," she said mischievously.

"Oh, right, because without your *expert* guidance, my life is one big wreck waiting to happen," I said, but I was teasing and we both knew it.

"Darn straight," she said. "Now get up, get dressed, and get downstairs. My furniture is being delivered today and that hot man you're all worried about is gonna be working right here under our roof all day."

Now that was motivation if I ever heard it.

After spending a little more time than usual getting dressed, I went downstairs anticipating a really good-looking guy, not a thoroughly ticked off one. Mark Haskell, my contractor, was standing in the center of the shop talking to Chase. Mark's arms were crossed defensively over his chest, and as I came within earshot I heard him say, "She could have just said she wanted someone else to do it."

"Do what?" I asked, honestly perplexed. "And good morning."

"Morning," Mark grumbled. Then he looked over my shoulder and said, "Hey, Tori."

"Hey, Mark," she answered. "Somebody take a leak in your Post Toasties this morning?"

"Very funny," Mark said, turning serious. "If you wanted to get someone else to do the downstairs bathroom, that's your choice, but you could have at least let me put in a counter bid."

I had no earthly idea what he was talking about. "I didn't hire anybody to do the bathroom," I said.

"Really, Jinx?" Mark said. "You honestly expect me to believe that?"

Beside him, Chase bristled. "I know I didn't just hear

you call the lady a liar, did I?" he said, putting a kind of menacingly chivalrous undertone on the question.

Great. Just what I needed. Testosterone drama at this hour of the day.

"Mark," I tried again, "I really don't know what you're talking about."

Just then Beau materialized behind the two men and supplied the answer, which only Tori and I could hear.

"Darby was trying to be helpful," the Colonel said. "He had no idea your contractor would react with such . . . territoriality."

Yeah, that's one way to put it.

Time to go into improv mode.

I feigned cluing in to what was going on. I almost slapped my head, but decided that was a little over the top.

"*Oh!*" I said, putting way too much emphasis on the word. "Are you talking about the cleaning service I hired? Did they do a good job?"

Shooting me a dubious look, Mark said, "You tell me." He strode over to the bathroom door and flung it open.

What's the next level up from immaculate?

Darby had transformed the dingy old bathroom into sparkling brilliance. Fresh paint covered the walls, and the fixtures were so spotless I swear there were those little starbursts glinting off the high spots like you see in staged photos.

"Uh, *wow*," I stalled.

"Are you telling me a *cleaning* service did this?" Mark demanded.

Okay. This whole outraged manhood thing was getting a little old. He was starting to sound like I'd stepped out on him with the Tidy Bowl man.

"Yes, *Mark*," I answered, putting a little sarcastic stress on his name. "That's exactly what I'm telling you. Take a look at the fixtures yourself. There's not one new piece of hardware in there."

God, I hoped I was right about that.

We watched as Mark walked in the bathroom and stooped over to look at the toilet. Then he got down on his hands and knees and examined the pipes, finally taking a small magnifying glass out of his pants pocket. At least five minutes passed before he leaned back and said, "Well, I will just be damned."

Quietly letting out the breath I'd been holding, I said. "I told them if they found anything loose they could tighten it up." It was a tiny embellishment on an already not-quite-lie, but I didn't push it any farther. "Other than that, they just cleaned," I said, trying to look like an innocent and satisfied customer.

"Well," he said grudgingly, "you got your money's worth and I am out a remodel. This place will pass inspection with flying colors."

Out of the corner of my eye, I saw Darby peering at me anxiously from inside a stack of apple crates I used to display soap.

"Fantastic," I said, purely for his benefit. "I'll be sure to tell the guy who did the cleaning that his work is first rate."

From the depths of the display, Darby flashed me a relieved smile.

"So," I said, trying for levity, "is there any other reason you're here on a Saturday, Mark, or did you just show up to rant about my bathroom."

He had the good grace to look sheepish. "Sorry," he said. "I just dropped by to bring Chase some finishing nails and paint. I didn't mean to pitch a fit."

I wanted to say, "You mean you didn't intend on acting like a big baby with hurt feelings," but I stopped myself. Just take the win, Jinx.

"Okay," I said, "then let's start over. Good morning, guys."

Both men grinned and we all exchanged second good mornings, which led to a little small talk about how the day's work would go. Tori's furniture delivery was set for 10 A.M. She and Chase disappeared into the new micro apartment out back to discuss placement, and Mark excused himself to get to another job.

When I knew I was alone in the front of the store, I said, "You can come out now, Darby."

The little man was suddenly just standing there in front of me. "I am sorry I made that man angry, Mistress," the brownie said, sounding worried. "I overheard that the repair of the bathroom was an impediment to your plans for the coffee house, so I thought I would help."

"You did help, Darby," I said sincerely, "and I very much appreciate it."

He looked like a puppy that had just been forgiven for piddling on the rug.

"You do?" he said, his face lighting up. "Oh, thank you, Mistress. May I make you a cup of coffee?"

"Yes, you may," I said.

Okay, sue me. I was starting to like having an accommodating magical creature in the house.

Darby's tiny form disappeared immediately. I'd given Chase a key so he could get started early, which meant the front door was already open. I quickly swept off the sidewalk and was looking at my email when a cup of coffee appeared on the table beside me. Darby had the whole "unobtrusive service" thing down pat.

Fortunately, I had taken a sip and put the cup back down when a voice on the other side of the counter said, "Jinx, honey, do you think you're drinking too much of that stuff?"

I looked up to find Aunt Fiona's ghost standing in front of me.

My first impulse was to fling my arms around her neck, but then I remembered that I was mad at her.

"Now you show up?" I asked crossly.

"Don't use that tone with me, dear," Aunt Fiona said pleasantly. "It makes you sound like your mother, and I don't think you want that, now do you?"

She had me there.

"I could have used your help in the cemetery the other night," I hissed, keeping my voice low. "Where were you *then*?"

Fiona seemed to give the question some thought and then said, "Monte Carlo, I think."

"I am not interested in your jet setting afterlife," I shot back tersely. "I need you to tell me how to undo this mess."

"I'm afraid I can't do that," Aunt Fiona said, still smiling beatifically, "but I can tell you more of the story than what Darby recounted last night."

Fantastic.

My dead aunt wasn't giving me a shred of help, but she *was* eavesdropping.

Fiona opened her mouth to go on, but I held up my hand.

"No," I said, "not now. This isn't just about me anymore. Tori is right in the middle of this mess, too, and so is Colonel Longworth and Darby. You can just come back tonight when we're all here alone and say whatever you have to say then."

"Well," Aunt Fiona huffed, "aren't you in a mood. I may have been mistaken in my assumption about that coffee. If I were you, I'd drink another couple of cups before dealing with any customers. You're downright surly, Norma Jean Hamilton."

And with that completely unwelcome use of my Christian name, she was gone.

"You better be back!" I hissed, a little louder than I intended.

"Did you say something, Jinksy?" Tori called from the back of the shop.

"No," I called back, "just talking to myself."

FOURTEEN

The rest of the day actually passed with blessed normalcy. The deliverymen arrived on time, and between Chase and Tori both giving them the eagle eye, everything was carried in and put in place with no mishaps. Chase supervised the assembly of the Murphy bed, which fit perfectly into the recessed spot Mark had created for it, and also put together the combination shelving unit / stairs that led up to the tiny loft Tori called her "chick cave."

Even though I knew Aunt Fiona was supposed to be back that evening, I didn't feel right not asking Chase to stay for supper. The three of us shared pizza and beer in Tori's new digs and talked for a while before Chase unsuccessfully tried to hide a massive yawn.

Coloring a little, he said, "Sorry. It's not the company. Just a long day."

"Us, too," I agreed, seizing the opportunity. "Maybe we should all call this one done."

He reluctantly agreed and Tori volunteered to clean everything up while I walked Chase to the door. The front of the store was lit only by the glow of the storeroom lamp. Chase put his arms around me, and said, "Hi, there."

Smiling up at him, I said, "Don't you have that backwards? We're supposed to be saying good night."

"Things have been so crazy with your remodel we

haven't had a chance to talk in forever," he said. "Take a bike ride with me tomorrow?"

Since I had no idea what Aunt Fiona would drop on us tonight, I couldn't commit to anything, but I really didn't want to say no. Chase saw the indecision on my face and came to the rescue.

"Or any day this week," he said, amending the invitation. "The weather is supposed to be pretty and it won't be hot. One day after work?"

"Yes," I said, smiling up at him. "And thank you. For everything."

"Thank you," he said, leaning down and kissing me.

When I had turned the lock behind him and heard him go into his own shop next door, I called out to Tori. "Okay, the coast is clear."

She emerged from the back of the store. Earlier in the day I'd managed to pull her aside and briefly explain that Aunt Fiona would be coming to call tonight.

"So what time is Fiona supposed to be here?" Tori asked.

"I have no idea," I answered. Turning to the shadows, I said, "Beau, are you around?"

The Colonel's pale form walked out of thin air and bowed. "At your service, Miss Jinx."

It occurred to me that he might have just had a front row seat for my goodnight kiss, but I decided I didn't really want to know.

"Darby?" I called out.

"Yes, Mistress?" the brownie said, materializing beside Beau.

Before I could say anything else, Aunt Fiona called out from the storeroom. "In here, Jinx, dear," she said. "Hurry up now. We have a lot to cover."

When the four of us joined her, we found my late aunt seated in one of the easy chairs feeding apple slices to Rodney. Now that I knew about Myrtle's solidifying effect on ghosts, I understood how my aunt managed to do things like pet my cats and move items in the store . . .

Wait a minute.

I looked around the storeroom. "What have you been doing in here, Aunt Fiona?" I demanded.

"Why, putting things back where they belong, dear," she said complacently. "You had the herbal stock in a terrible mess."

"We had the herbs in terrible *organization*," Tori broke in, grinning. "Hi, Auntie Fi."

"Tori!" Fiona cried happily. "You come here and hug my neck!"

Tori went over automatically, then hesitated, arms in mid-air. "Is this gonna work?" she asked.

"Of course it is," Fiona said, smothering her in a maternal hug.

After a moment of brief surprise at the low-temperature embrace, Tori said, "Wow! You're going to be better than a Popsicle on a hot summer day."

Fiona giggled. Then she caught sight of Beau and a shy look came over her cheerful features. "Good evening, Colonel Longworth," she said.

Hold the phone. Fiona actually batted her eyes at him . . . demurely, no less.

"Miss Fiona," Beau said, beaming. As Tori and I watched, the old soldier kissed my aunt's hand, which elicited another giggle from Fiona. As he stood upright again, Beau said, "I have been waiting many years for the pleasure of that greeting. Death quite agrees with you, Fiona. You look lovely."

That's when I realized Beau and Fiona had never seen each other outside of the graveyard, nor had they ever been on equal . . . footing. As in both dead.

Could they possibly be sweet on each other? Somehow

that whole notion struck me as impossibly cute and thoroughly endearing. My annoyance at my aunt dialed down several levels.

From behind Beau, Darby said shyly, "It is an honor to meet you, Mistress Fiona."

Fiona smiled at the brownie kindly and gestured for him to come closer. Standing in front of her chair, the little guy was still too short to look her in the eye. "What is your name?" she asked.

Darby let out the same multi-consonant cat yack he'd given me in the cemetery and then added helpfully, "But Mistress Jinx has directed me to answer to the name Darby," he dropped his eyes. "I like it," he added.

"So do I, Master Darby," Fiona said. "Are you happy to be here with Myrtle?"

His head bobbed up and down, and he rewarded my aunt with an ecstatic smile. "Very happy, Mistress."

"Okay," I said, "let's just start there. What's the deal with Myrtle and Darby?"

Fiona patted the seat cushion and Darby settled in happily beside her. "The store," she said, "is built on an ancient fairy mound. Myrtle is the life force of that dwelling. To Darby and to many other magical creatures, she is a queen."

The look on my face must have given away my reaction to that bit of news

"Don't worry," Fiona went on. "They're not the kind of creatures you've been reading about on those silly Internet sites. The correct term would be 'lesser fae,' but I really don't have time to explain all that to you right now. All you need to know is that Myrtle is completely on our side, even if she did get ridiculously testy about that whole painting business."

From somewhere over our heads, the store blew Fiona a raspberry.

Without missing a beat, my aunt looked up and said, "I do agree with you about the cerulean blue, however."

That won her one of Myrtle's three-note trills.

Since I was sensing that this could be the start of one, great-big designer rabbit trail, I said, "Okay. As fascinating as this whole metaphysical Martha Stewart conversation might be, could we please deal with the bigger crisis at hand?"

"Which one, dear?" Aunt Fiona asked, looking over at me innocently.

"*Really*, Fiona?" I said, getting a little testy myself.

She sighed. "Oh, alright. I guess you mean Brenna Sinclair."

"Uh, *yeah*," I replied. "I'd say she kinda qualifies as a crisis."

Fiona shifted over to make more room for Darby. "Well, you see, Jinx, there's a great deal I have to tell you before I can actually talk about Brenna herself."

"Then get to talking," I said. "We have all night."

Little did I know we were going to need the whole night.

If Darby's recitation the evening before had left us all a little stunned, this one made me feel like we'd just signed up for Defense Against the Dark Arts at Hogwarts. The only thing that saved me was the Southern preoccupation with genealogy. Yes, my mother forced me to fill out an application to join the Daughters of the Confederacy, and no, I do not own a hoop skirt.

The most important question Fiona answered for us that night was: Are you a good witch or a bad witch? More to the point: Are you a made witch or an hereditary witch. If you're getting a whole *Godfather* "Luca-sleeps-with-the-fishes" vibe off the term "made witch" you're already on the right track.

Darby knew the broad strokes of Brenna's story, but

Fiona filled in the details. Long before Brenna ever met Hamish Crawford, she was a human woman who made a deal with a dark entity in exchange for her powers. The exact details of this arrangement fell under Fiona's "I don't have time for that" imprimatur, but we did learn that there are folks out there called "dark fae," and we don't want on their radar, ever.

Even though Fiona was vague on the exact timeline, I could well imagine that whatever Brenna's life had been before forging that deal, it wasn't good. The lady was out for some serious payback. To get it, she sacrificed her humanity, and her ability to bear children. That is until she hooked up with Hamish Crawford.

The child she carried was her opportunity to form her own line of hereditary witches. You see, by definition, made witches are "bad," but hereditary witches are "good," in that their line of descent traces back to original, pure, earth magic. There was a part of Brenna that wanted to legitimize who and what she was, but the lengths she was willing to go to in the process were anything but legitimate.

Duncan Skea was himself a witch, or more a kind of Druid. I'm iffy on the exact wording on his business card, but he definitely had the chops to imprison Brenna. Her child only had half metaphysical blood, and sort of *synthetic* blood at that. If they could just keep her locked up for enough generations, the magic Brenna passed to her child would dissipate.

At the point at which she escaped, and Fiona had no answer to that mystery either, Alexander Skea carried only about 12.5% magic. The Skeas carefully chose brides for Alistair and Angus for the express purpose of diluting their magic. But then Alexander came to the New World and fell in love with a full-blooded Cherokee witch.

I'll admit I didn't follow all the ancestral math Fiona

sketched out for us, but I can tell you that Alexander and Knasgowa's children had an even higher concentration of magic in their blood than Brenna's son, Alistair. Knasgowa's pure magic more or less reconstituted Brenna's magic.

But here was the major surprise behind door number three. When Alexander met Knasgowa, she already had a three-year-old daughter from her first husband, a Cherokee medicine man killed in a hunting accident. That child, Awenasa, was my ancestor and her blood was 100% magical.

"Wait a minute," I said, interrupting my aunt. "You're telling me that we're hereditary *Cherokee* witches?"

"Only through Awenasa," Fiona said. "Most of our people are Scots who came into the Carolinas. But they carried Celtic magic in their blood."

"So how much magic is in my blood?" I asked.

Aunt Fiona thought for a minute and said, "Do you remember your high school biology?"

I remembered stoutly refusing to dissect anything and being in danger of flunking until my teacher took pity on me and cut me a deal. I graded all his papers that year in exchange for no lab time involving deceased animals.

"Kinda," I said. "Why?"

"Did your teacher talk to you kids about genetics?" Fiona asked.

Some vague memory of little tic-tac-toe diagrams of dominant and recessive traits surfaced in my mind. When I told Aunt Fiona that, she said, "Okay, that's good enough. So, look at it this way. Magic can be either a dominant or a recessive gene. So it comes out with varying degrees of strength, but if you get two dominant genes, then you get a really strong witch. Does that make sense, dear?"

I nodded. "Yeah, but what does that have to do with me?"

"Neither of your parents is magical in their own right," Fiona said. "In fact, Kelly refused to have anything to do with the family legacy. That's why she's always called me crazy."

Ouch! I didn't know Fiona actually *knew* that the family called her "Crazy Aunt Fiona."

Then another thought t-boned my discomfort.

"My *mother* knows about all this stuff?" I asked, shocked.

"Yes," Fiona said complacently, "but she is the original queen of denial."

Beside me Tori snickered and sang a few bars of "Dance Like an Egyptian." I shot her a look and she hushed.

"So if Mom and Dad aren't magical, how come I am? Just because you gave me my magic?" I asked Fiona.

"I didn't actually give it to you, dear," Fiona said. "I activated it. Your parents each gave you a dominant gene for magic. You have the potential to be the most powerful witch our family has seen in generations." My aunt looked at me, her eyes shining. "I couldn't be more proud of you if I tried."

I cannot even begin to tell you how much happier I would have been at that moment if she had been proud of me for *any* other reason.

Beside me, Tori's fertile brain had been at work. "So, let me take a wild guess here," she said. "There are still descendants of Alexander and Knasgowa's around Briar Hollow that carry Brenna's genes."

"Yes," Fiona nodded.

"Just like you all carry Knasgowa's magic from her first husband," Tori went on.

Fiona nodded again. "Exactly."

"And I'm betting that your side of the family is part of the whole plan to keep the other side of the family on their best behavior," Tori finished.

"Very good," Fiona beamed. "That's it precisely. The Briar Hollow coven has helped to guard Knasgowa's grave since her death.

Whoa! What the *what*?! Did she just say *coven*?

"There's a Briar Hollow coven?" I asked weakly.

Fiona shook her head sadly. "Not anymore. I'm afraid we're all gone now."

"Which means what for me?" I asked, dreading what I already knew she was going to say.

"Why, it means you have to start over, dear," Fiona said.

Great. The one "do over" I *didn't* want.

FIFTEEN

Start over?

How the heck was I supposed to start over?

Put an ad in the *Banner*?

"Wanted. Thirteen women with magical blood to form coven. Must supply pointy hats. Made witches need not apply."

Fiona laughed merrily at my suggestion.

"Oh, Jinx," she said, "thank heavens you inherited a sense of humor from your father."

That's me, alright. A laugh a minute.

"Fine, no witchy want ads," I said. "What *am* I supposed to do? *Specifically*."

Fiona looked uncomfortable as she admitted, sheepishly, "Jinx, I want you to know I do feel some responsibility for all this. I have been sort of preoccupied with my new afterlife and I *might* have left you a little unprepared, but I really had no earthly idea you'd set Brenna free."

Okay. Time to derail the blame train.

"I didn't do it on purpose," I said crossly. "I was trying to help the spirits trapped in the graveyard, and it's not like there was some big sign on Knasgowa's grave that said, 'Danger. Evil Sorceress Imprisoned Here.'"

"Well, no, dear," Aunt Fiona said reasonably. "That would be a little obvious, don't you think?"

Man. You have no idea how nice it would be to have some *obvious* to deal with.

Rightly interpreting my scowl, Fiona added hastily, "Honestly, Jinx, I really haven't thought about Brenna in years. I mean, I knew she was *there*, but she wasn't on my mind every day or anything like that. Really, sugar, I had every good intention of filling you in on the big picture once you got used to your powers."

Good intention, meet road to hell.

"You haven't *thought* about her?" I gasped, looking at my aunt in total amazement. "How is that even *possible*?"

"Jinx, for heaven's sake," she said, starting to sound a little exasperated herself, "be realistic. Nothing ever happens in Briar Hollow. Knasgowa was buried in 1853. The local coven has been responsible for guarding her grave for 262 *uneventful* years."

Okay. Now I really was confused. Just what exactly had Team Witch been doing all that time?

"So you were a coven in name only?" I asked.

"Oh, no, not at all, " Fiona said brightly. "We read books together and sponsored one of the local Little League teams. Baked cakes for shut ins. Had potluck solstice suppers. You know. The usual."

Tori broke in at this point. "You actually sponsored a Little League team?" she asked, obviously fascinated. "What did you all have printed on the back of the uniforms?"

"The Ladies Circle," Fiona said earnestly. "You can get away with almost anything if you just call yourselves a 'circle.'"

Colonel Longworth, who was sitting on the loveseat with Tori, burst out laughing.

"And just what do you think is so funny about all this?" I asked.

Still grinning, he said, "She's right. My wife was part of a Ladies Circle. They read political literature, covertly supported abolition, and debated Mr. Lincoln's policies, all the while claiming to be crocheting."

Tori frowned. "What's unusual about a bunch of women talking politics?"

"In my day," Beau said, "ladies were not supposed to concern their . . ." He stopped mid-sentence, looking distinctly like a deer caught in the headlights.

"Pretty little heads," I supplied helpfully, cocking an eyebrow in his direction.

"Yes," he admitted reluctantly. Then added quickly, "Not that I believed . . . er, believe that the fairer . . . uh, that women lack . . ."

Beside him Tori advised, "You might want to stop digging that hole there, Beau. You're getting in pretty deep."

The wisecrack broke the awkwardness and underlying tension in the room. We all laughed, even little Darby.

"Okay, Aunt Fiona," I said, regaining my composure, "I get it. Out of sight, out of mind. But Brenna is very much in sight now. And you said I need to start over, so exactly what did you mean by that?"

"Well," Fiona said, "not to be overly simplistic, but you need to put her back where you found her and develop a new circle of guardians. Having magical associations helps a witch keep her own powers in balance, you know."

I wasn't a hundred percent certain, but I was pretty sure my aunt had just told me to get a social life.

"Let's try this again," I said. "*How* do I put Brenna back?"

"I have no idea," Fiona said.

This whole conversation was starting to make me feel like I was running circles in Rodney's rat wheel.

"Your coven didn't come with a set of instructions?" I demanded. "The combination to the tombstone? *Something*?"

Fiona gave me a slightly more benevolent version of "the look" my mom used when I fidgeted in church.

"Don't you get uppity with me, Jinx Hamilton," she said. "Our job was to make sure no one disturbed the grave. No one did. Until you decided to get too big for your britches and start casting spells."

Now that really annoyed me. I don't mind owning up to my mistakes, but this was getting old. I felt the heat rise to my face, and then the temperature in the room went up. The magazines on the coffee table levitated a few inches and the hands of the wall clock started spinning like a roulette wheel.

I opened my mouth to really tear into my aunt, but before I could say anything, I felt Tori's hand on my arm. My head snapped toward her, but she never so much as flinched. Lightning bolts could have been shooting out of my fingertips and Tori wouldn't be scared of me.

"Simmer *down*, Jinksy," she commanded. "You'll never forgive yourself if you hurt somebody."

Just like that, my anger was gone.

This was the first time since my powers awakened that I'd come even close to losing my temper, which at most happens once or twice a year anyway. I'm like my Dad; we have super long fuses, but when we finally do pitch a fit, everybody and God knows it.

"Sorry," I said weakly. "I didn't mean to get all scary on you all."

"No," Aunt Fiona said apologetically, "I'm the one who should be apologizing. I shouldn't have said that about you getting too big for your britches."

Beau cleared his throat. "If I may?" he asked.

"By all means," I said. "I'm open to any ideas at this point."

"If I am following the course of your narrative correctly, Fiona," the Colonel said, "you and your associates were to guard the grave for signs of trouble, but you were not to act in the event of such an instance?"

"Not exactly," Fiona said. "If something were to happen, we were to consult Alexander Skea's private diary."

Finally. Progress.

"Great!" I jumped in. "So where's the book?"

Fiona hesitated. "That's the part I haven't wanted to tell you," she said.

I just looked at her, waiting.

"The diary was buried with him," she said.

Okay. That wasn't so bad. We could dig up a dead guy. In the greater scheme of things, we could be asked to do much worse. In fact, I think we already *had* done worse.

"Fine," I said. "So we dig. Where is he?"

"I don't know," Fiona said.

Are you *kidding* me?

"Fiona," I groaned, "seriously?"

"It's not my fault!" she protested. "I didn't tell Rita Louise Sorrell to choke on a peach pit."

Well, that explained everything. Not.

Putting my hand over my eyes and shaking my head, I said, "In English, please?"

"Only one member of the coven was entrusted with the location of Alexander's grave," Fiona answered. "That was Rita Louise Sorrell. She was supposed to pass the information to her daughter, but she didn't have one, so Rita Louise was going to pick one of us, and before she could, she choked to death at her kitchen table on a peach pit. It was just *awful*, Jinx. Nobody found her for two or three days and it was summer time . . ."

"Stop!" I ordered.

The last thing I needed to hear about was the details of Rita Louise Sorrell ripening up in the summer heat.

Aunt Fiona clamped her mouth shut and Darby put his hand up as if asking for permission to speak.

"You don't have to raise your hand, Darby," I said, smiling in spite of myself. "What is it?"

"Her Majesty told me that you have the power of sight?" he said, making the statement a question.

"Yes," I said, " I can touch objects and see things in the past. Why?"

"Couldn't you touch something that belonged to Master Alexander and see his last days?"

Well. Score one for the munchkin.

"Darby," I said, grinning, "you're brilliant!"

The little brownie fairly glowed with pleasure.

"Okay," Tori said, "how do we find Alexander Skea's stuff? Assuming any of it is still around."

"It's a long shot," Fiona said, "but you might try the Briar Hollow Historical Association. They share space with the library on the other side of the square. The librarian, Linda Albert, is also the head of the historical association."

Perfect. I already knew Linda. She helped me find old copies of the Briar Hollow High School yearbook when I first came to town and had a teenage ghost with amnesia on my hands.

It might not have sounded like the start of a grand adventure, but it looked like we were about to hit the books.

"I'll go over there in the morning," I said, glancing at the clock and then remembering what I'd done to the hands. I looked at Tori. "What time is it?"

She glanced at her wristwatch. "Not quite 1 o'clock."

I looked at my aunt. "Do you have anything else you want to tell me before we call it a night?" I asked.

Fiona shook her head. "No, I don't think so."

"You're sure?" I pressed.

"I can't imagine what it would be," Aunt Fiona said innocently.

Please don't think badly of me, but I didn't believe a word of it.

SIXTEEN

The way I shared this last part of the story, it sounds like accidentally making magazines levitate and clock hands spin didn't freak me out. Not so much. It's just that with everything else that was going on, I had to keep it together until I got upstairs.

After Aunt Fiona excused herself to "see if I can catch the girls in Reno," and Beau went to check on his friends among the cemetery regulars, Tori and I were left in the storeroom with Darby. The little brownie looked up at me expectantly and said, "Mistress Jinx, may I have permission to clean and organize the basement?"

Yeah. We haven't talked about the basement yet. Right after I inherited the store, I opened the door to go down there, hitting the light switch from the top step. Think warehouse at the end of the Indiana Jones movie. Since I was already overwhelmed by the lack of inventory control up top, I had no interest in descending further into chaos—and chaos with the likely presence of spiders at that.

"It's all yours, Darby," I said. "Do your thing."

With profuse thanks, the little guy winked out. That's when Tori and I took a minute to check the library's hours on the county website. To our surprise, it was open on Sunday afternoons, but well after all local church services had concluded for the day and the lunch run at the cafe was over. We didn't have to walk across the square until 1 o'clock.

Tori was spending her first night in the new apartment. I walked her to her "front door," which was actually just to the left of the door leading into the alley. In typical Tori fashion, she painted it red (with no objections from Myrtle) and put down a zombie apocalypse welcome mat. It features two footprints in a blood splatter and the caption reads, "Welcome to Tori's. Bring Your Own Brains."

Giving my BFF a hug, I said, "Congrats on the new place. Don't stay up half the night organizing your books in the Chick Cave."

"I won't," she promised. "This business of being up until all hours talking to dead people is starting to wear me out, too. At least we don't have to get up at the crack of dawn in the morning."

As I turned away from Tori's door to go upstairs, she called out my name in a questioning tone.

When I looked back, she was leaning against the doorframe. "You gonna be okay up there by yourself?" she asked.

"I have four cats," I pointed out. "I am never alone."

Not even in the bathroom.

My fellow crazy cat ladies will totally understand that statement.

"You know what I mean," Tori said. "That *thing* you did in there with the magazines and the clock was kinda intense. I know you."

Sometimes she knows me too well.

Blowing out a long breath, I said, "Yeah, ya think? I had no idea that could happen."

"You want to talk about it?"

I shook my head. "I need to think about it for awhile."

"It's not helping that getting intel out of Fiona is like pulling teeth with tweezers, is it?" Tori said.

God, that was putting it mildly.

"Do you think she's being vague on purpose?" I asked.

"I think she's just being Aunt Fiona," Tori said, "using Aunt Fiona logic. She always has been an outside-the-box kinda gal."

I shook my head. "That was fine when it came to keeping a crazy inventory in the store," I said, "but we're playing with some serious stuff here."

"We'll figure it out," Tori said with conviction.

"How can you be so sure about that?" I countered.

"Because we always do," she replied.

Yeah, I know. You read that and it sounds all silly and trite, but when you're looking at someone with whom you share a lifelong history of "figuring it out," an assurance like that can be pretty danged comforting.

"Go," I grinned. "I know you're dying to alphabetize your *Star Trek* novels before you go to sleep."

She rolled her eyes. "You don't alphabetize sci fi, Jinksy. You organize by season and episode arc."

I held my hands up in front of my face and backed away. "May the Force be with you," I said.

"That's *Star Wars*, not *Star Trek*, dufus," she said.

I knew that, and she knew that I knew that, but sometimes you just give your BFF an opening for the heck of it.

As I headed to my place alone, I admit I had a little anxious pang at the top of the stairs, but it wasn't like I couldn't go back down and wake Tori up if I needed anything. She was right, though. I was having a hard time turning my mind off.

In the roughly two months I'd been a witch, a great deal of my time had been spent in (a) denial, (b) reluctant acceptance, (c) fear of hellfire and damnation, (d) meandering self-study, (e) all of the above.

E. Final answer.

See how easy it is to pass a multiple-choice test?

Of all my abilities, I liked talking to ghosts the best. Before Brenna, I only had one scary encounter and that was with a girl who had been murdered by a serial killer and dumped in the woods. She had every right to be cranky.

The telekinesis (moving stuff with my mind) was just downright handy. But truth be told, up to that point I had mainly used that one to avoid having to reach for the remote control. The psychometry, getting visions from touching something, still scared me a little. The power had allowed me to hear the voice of an ancient hickory tree, which was beyond cool but also completely life altering.

I was just beginning to understand that "magic" is another word for what someone else might call "life force" or "universal intelligence." The amount of information you can jack into with magic makes the Internet read like a fortune cookie. I'm an ex-waitress with a high school diploma. Sure, I've always had my head poked in a book, but there are moments when I seriously wonder if I'm smart enough to handle all this.

There's just so much to understand and try to remember! It should have occurred to me that my powers might get unpredictable if I was angry or upset, or really just exhausted and impatient. That's a better description for what I'd been feeling downstairs.

As these thoughts were roaming around in my head, I walked over to the front window to look out on the courthouse square. We hadn't done anything to get the ghosts back in their graves, so it looked like the set of *Night at the Museum* out there for the third night in a row.

That's when I saw Howard McAlpin standing—or rather floating—on top of the cannon by the Confederate memorial speaking to a milling crowd of ghosts gathering below.

Just. Freaking. Great.

This guy simply would not get it through his thick, transparent skull that he'd run his last race. Or so I thought.

I'd already changed into my favorite pajamas emblazoned with unicorns and rainbows, so I threw on the old denim shirt of my dad's I usually reserve for Sunday TV binge watching on the couch. The sleeves are so long, I deal with a thick roll of fabric at each wrist and the tail of the shirt almost reaches my knees.

I assure you that in no way did I look like either the voice of reason or authority when I charged out the front door of the store and marched over to the monument.

As I came within earshot, I heard Howard say, "Do you want to be like those mindless spirits in the graveyard following the leadership of a slave-holding tyrant and a traitor to these great United States? I am campaigning on a platform of afterlife emancipation. We did not give up our fundamental rights of life, liberty, and the pursuit of happiness just because we died."

And that, ladies and gentlemen, is the oxymoron of the century uttered by a political moron. American politics at its best.

"Howie," I hissed sternly, "you get yourself down here right *now*."

McAlpin's expression turned to one of self-righteous triumph. "You see, ladies and gentlemen? There she is. The unholy agent of the repressive dead."

What did that even *mean*?

The spirits turned toward me, a kind of anxious, half-angry muttering rippling through their glowing forms. I was *so* not in the mood for this. Remember that one angry ghost I told you about? Well, in dealing with her, I had learned a little trick. I could reverse my telekinesis.

As the specters moved toward me, I raised my hand and focused my thoughts. A circle of blue light formed about six inches in front of my fingers. I pushed a little and it expanded into a sphere.

"Back. Up."

The order came out of my mouth with just the right amount of bitchy terseness.

Most of the ghosts stopped, but one guy, who just *had* to have been a Baptist preacher in life, kept coming.

"I will not be cowed by you, you evil Jezebel," he said.

Okay. *Jezebel.* Cool movie. And you're gonna think "cow," buddy.

I didn't even hit him hard. It was just a little metaphysical love tap, but down he went—and immediately started scrambling back on all fours, which was pretty funny since he had no solid physical form. He stopped about six feet back with a fire hydrant sticking out of his chest.

"I said, back up," I repeated. "Do I have to tell you again?"

The guy shook his head so hard it looked like a whirling gray funnel cloud.

"Good," I said, turning to the others. "Now, break it up. Howie is done for the night. You all go find something else to do."

As I watched, the spirits all floated away, some of them casting worried glances back at me. When I turned my attention toward the monument, Howard McAlpin was standing in front of me.

"You cannot intimidate my constituency that way," he said. "It's voter intimidation."

Un-freaking-believable.

"As much as I hate to ask this question, Howie," I said, enjoying the way he flinched when I used the nickname, "exactly what do you think you're doing?"

Puffing himself up like a preening rooster, he said, "Democratizing the dead."

Clearly this guy had no concept of voter apathy.

"Uh huh," I said. "Democratizing them to do what exactly?"

"To oust that Confederate traitor from his dictatorship at the cemetery," Howie replied with carefully crafted faux indignation.

I took a step toward him. "You say one more word against Beau Longworth and you're getting a lightning bolt right up your ectoplasmic backside."

From behind me I heard a thinly disguised chuckle, followed by a clucking sound. "Now, Miss Jinx," Beau said, "remember your manners."

"I am not feeling like a paragon of Southern womanhood at the moment, Beau," I answered, without looking back.

The Colonel floated up beside me and regarded McAlpin. "Good evening, Mr. Mayor," he said pleasantly. "That was quite a rousing bit of political oratory."

"Oh, sure," McAlpin snapped. "Don't pull that gallant Southern gentleman thing with me. No wonder those ghosts have been trapped in that graveyard all these years. You like having your slaves, don't you, buddy?"

I was pretty sure Howard McAlpin had never given the history of civil rights so much as a thought until it could be a political tool for whatever the heck he had in mind, but before I could say anything, Beau spoke.

"Upon the death of my father," the Colonel said gravely, "I emancipated our people and gave them parcels of land so they might support themselves. I did not participate in the Late Unpleasantness in support of slavery. While I understand that you could not have known these facts prior to this conversation, I would appreciate the cessation of attacks upon my character."

Even Howie couldn't come up with a wise ass crack in the face of that one. Some things do endure after death. Integrity is on the list. I'll give the bombastic runt this; Howard did have the grace to apologize.

"I'm sorry," he said, even though it looked like he was about to choke on the words. "But I still think the ghosts of Briar Hollow are in crying need of real leadership."

What the ghosts of Briar Hollow—or at least most of them—really needed was a good long nap. Like for eternity.

I opened my mouth to say something, but Beau interrupted me. "May I have a word with you in private, Miss Jinx?"

We stepped away a few paces and the Colonel lowered his voice. "Let Mr. McAlpin have his fun," he said. "He can do me no harm."

"He's a rabble rousing little . . ." I started.

"I do not disagree," Beau said, "but that is all he can do, and this ridiculous campaign is keeping him occupied."

Oh.

Which meant one less thing I had to deal with.

Good point.

Before I could answer, McAlpin called out to us. "You two can conspire all you like," he said, "but this is America, and I will not be silenced."

Putting on my best "concerned citizen" face, I said, "You're absolutely right, Howard. Who am I to try to deny the dead their civil rights?"

I don't know what shocked McAlpin more, the fact that I didn't taunt him with the detested nickname or that I seemed to be agreeing with him.

"Well," he huffed. "Well, that's . . . more . . . like it."

With witty repartee of that quality, no wonder this guy went into politics. But Howie wasn't done yet.

"And I'll tell you another thing," he blustered, "I *will* have my murder avenged."

"I would expect no less of a man of your noble disposition," Beau said smoothly. "The pursuit of justice is clearly an ideal near and dear to your heart."

Howard's brow furrowed. He couldn't tell if Beau was being sincere or not, but finally decided to err on the side of dignity—his own.

"Exactly," the mayor said with studied finality. "Couldn't have said it better myself."

That was the opening I'd been looking for. "Well, we won't keep you, Mr. Mayor," I said pleasantly. "I know you have a lot of work to do."

Howard picked up on the brush-off, but he couldn't really object without making it look like he had no reason for existing, which he kind of didn't. He gave each of us a curt little nod and went striding off across the courthouse lawn fairly pulsating with self-importance.

"That should take care of him for a while," Beau said. "I think you have more than enough on your hands for the moment."

Seriously. I'm getting him one of those t-shirts that reads, "Got understatement?"

SEVENTEEN

We treated ourselves to a lazy Sunday morning. Tori asked me to come down to her place for breakfast. We ate at the convertible coffee table in the tiny living room, keeping the conversation light. I mentioned that the micro apartment reminded me of our childhood tree house, which touched off a wave of happy nostalgia. I can't even begin to estimate how many hours we spent up in that old mulberry tree reading and dreaming of what we'd do when we grew up.

Not talking about ghosts and resurrected witches was the best thing we could have done. By the time I went upstairs to spend some quality time with the cats, I felt better than I had in days. Understand that when I say "quality time" I mean that I sprawled on the couch to watch *Jessica Jones* on Netflix with Winston, Xavier, Yule, and Zeke sprawled on top of me. It's a sprawlage bonding thing with intermittent snoozing involved.

Fortunately I thought to set an alarm on my phone, so I made it downstairs on schedule just a little before 1 o'clock. To my surprise, Darby was waiting by the front door with Tori.

I shot her a raised eyebrow and she just shrugged, telegraphing the message "you deal with it" in nonverbal BFF speak. I supposed that was fair, since the little guy thought of me as more or less his employer.

126

"Uh, hi, Darby," I said. "Do you need something?"

"I am accompanying you to the library," he answered brightly.

This wasn't an idea he'd floated by us and I wasn't so sure it was a good one. Not wanting to hurt the little guy's feelings, I said neutrally, "Any particular reason why?"

Darby looked confused. "Aren't you planning to look for something that belonged to my master?" he asked.

"Yes," I said, "that's the idea."

"How will you know that what you find really belonged to him?" the brownie asked.

I have to admit that question hadn't occurred to me.

"I, uh, well, I guess I'll just pick it up and see if Alexander comes into to my mind," I said lamely.

"Do you know what my master looked like?" Darby asked.

By this time, Tori could no longer contain herself. She laughed. "He's got you dead to rights," she said. "I'd say he's riding shotgun."

Alarm filled Darby's features. "Please don't make me do that," he protested. "I am afraid of firearms."

Tori patted him on the shoulder. "That's not what 'riding shotgun' means," she said. "It's an expression for 'you're coming along.'"

He was instantly on board. "Oh, good," he said. "Then, please, may I ride the firearm?"

It's pretty much impossible to spend time with Darby and not fall in love with him. The non-sequiturs alone will do it.

"Yes," I said, looking down at him fondly, "you can come along, but you have to stay invisible and you can't talk if anyone else is nearby. Understand?"

Darby nodded enthusiastically and immediately popped out of sight.

The three of us walked across the courthouse lawn toward the library. As we passed the Confederate monument, Tori said, "So this is where Howie did the whole 'as God is my witness I'll never be dead again' speech?"

"Yep," I said, "floating right over the cannon."

"You have to admit that would make one heck of a campaign poster," she said.

"Do *not* encourage him," I warned.

When we walked in the building, the librarian, Linda Albert, greeted me by name, and I introduced her to Tori. We had already concocted our story. Tori claimed to be taking a history class with an online university. She was supposedly writing a paper on Scottish immigrants in the Carolinas and had gotten interested in Orkney Islanders in particular.

"I ran across the name 'Alexander Skea,'" she said, sounding as academic as a woman with magenta highlights can manage. "It was in a letter to his, uh, cousin, back in Scotland describing how he married a Cherokee woman who was from around here."

Linda frowned, making her half glasses bob up on her nose. "That's quite some story," she said. "If it's true, I can't imagine why I've never heard it. The name Skea is pretty unusual."

"I think his wife's name was Knasgowa," Tori supplied helpfully.

"Oh!" Linda said, snapping her fingers. "I do know about her. She's buried in the local cemetery under a real nice black tombstone. It's an unusual marker for the period. I think she died around 1850 or thereabouts. The stone doesn't give a last name though. That's the Alexander you're looking for?"

"I think so," Tori said. "Do you have any more information about her?"

Linda shook her head. "Not really," she said, "but

you're welcome to go through the files for the 1850s to see if you can come up with anything."

We followed her across the library and through a door emblazoned with a plaque that read "Briar Hollow Historical Association." Linda disappeared into the shelves and started carrying out boxes, giving us white gloves to wear while we handled the contents.

"You don't have to stay with us," I said, trying not to sound like I wanted her to leave, which I did. "We'll be super careful to keep everything in order."

Linda looked uncertain for a minute and then seemed to come to a decision—the right one.

"Okay," she said. "I wouldn't normally do this, but I trust you since you're Fiona's niece. I have an absolute ton of paperwork I need to get done today. If you all want coffee, just help yourselves to the machine in the front, but you can't bring any food and drink in here. Okay?"

We promised and waited until we could no longer hear her footsteps to say anything.

When I was sure we were in the clear, I asked, in a low tone, "Darby, are you still here?"

"Yes, Mistress," his disembodied voice said from the area to the left of my chair.

"Can you see the things we're looking at from down there?"

"No," he said. "I am not tall enough."

Without being asked, Tori moved a third chair to the table, setting it away from the edge. We waited until the chair wobbled slightly, indicating that Darby was in place, and then we began to go through the boxes.

There are far worse ways to spend a Sunday afternoon. We were both quickly engrossed by the letters, journals, and daguerreotypes in the boxes. Three hours passed, however, without one mention of Alexander and Knasgowa.

Then, at the very bottom of the sixth box I took out a picture of a group of men wearing Masonic aprons. Beside me, Darby gasped. "That is my master!" he said.

"Which one?" I asked.

Darby made himself visible and carefully pointed to a tall, handsome man in the back row. Alexander Skea stood head and shoulders over his Lodge brothers, looking at the camera with grave dignity, but there was also a glint in his eye that betrayed good humor.

On instinct, I turned the photo over, and sure enough, there were names penciled on the back. Alexander, however, was labeled "unknown."

"What was your master like, Darby?" I asked, suddenly curious.

The brownie stared wistfully at the photo. "Master Alexander was kind," he said finally, loving sadness filling his voice. "When he laughed the sun in the sky grew brighter."

"You miss him, don't you?" Tori asked.

"I miss Master Alexander *and* Mistress Knasgowa," Darby said. Then he looked at us with loyalty in his eyes. "But I am very happy in my new home."

See what I mean? Completely adorable *and* he loves to cook and clean. Put another 3 or 4 feet on Darby and he could be *Bachelor* material.

"Do you get any images off the photo?" Tori asked.

Closing my eyes, I cleared my mind, opening a space for impressions to enter and solidify, but there was nothing.

After several minutes, I shook my head and gave up. "Nothing," I said. "Maybe it's not working because the photo didn't actually belong to Alexander."

Tori chewed her lip and then something occurred to her. "Maybe it's the gloves," she suggested. "You know, blocking the signal or something?"

I peeled off the white gloves and gingerly picked up the photo again, holding it by the edges. The last thing I wanted to do was leave fingerprints.

As soon as my skin touched the aged cardboard, I felt a little frisson of energy, but when I closed my eyes, I didn't see Alexander Skea. Instead, I was in a Masonic Lodge hall during a ceremony. My eyes snapped open instantly and I dropped the picture.

"What happened?" Tori asked.

"I got an image of the Lodge hall," I answered. "I'm not supposed to be in there."

Both of our dads are Masons, so I knew the meetings are conducted in secret.

Okay, settle down. Don't go all conspiracy theory on me. Other than having fantastic potluck suppers and wearing silly hats if they go on to become Shriners, Masons are totally harmless.

My reaction to the fleeting vision was just a matter of my respecting a tradition kept by the men in my family. Besides, I'd had just enough time to glance around the meeting room in my mind. Alexander Skea hadn't been there.

We'd gone through all the boxes Linda brought out to us and it was after 4 o'clock. It didn't seem likely that we'd find anything else today, so Tori and I agreed to give up for the time being.

Before I returned the picture of Alexander and his Lodge brothers to the proper box, however, I took out my phone and snapped several photos front and back, including a close-up of Alexander himself.

To make sure the pictures were in focus, I quickly thumbed through them on the phone, only to stop when one name at the bottom of the list jumped out at me: James McGregor. It took some flipping back and forth, but I finally figured out that he was the man in in the center of the image. By his name, the letters "WM" indicated he had been the Worshipful Master or head of the Lodge at the time the group posed for the photo. Could he be Chase's ancestor?

We thanked Linda on our way out. Since the switch to Daylight Savings Time had already happened, which my dad calls "damned government time," there was still plenty of light left in the day.

As we approached the shop, Chase came out the front door wheeling his bike. He greeted me with a hopeful, "Sure you don't want to change your mind?"

I glanced at Tori, who gave me a meaningful look that fairly screamed, "Go!"

"Can you give me, like, 10 minutes to change and get my bike?" I asked.

Chase looked like he'd just won the lottery, which kinda made my heart do that "pitty patter" thing. The bike ride would be good exercise, but honestly? I can get all the cardio I need just looking at Chase McGregor.

"You bet!" he grinned. "Take as much time as you like. We have plenty of daylight left."

Most of my reason for running up and getting changed at lightning speed was the prospect of an outing with Chase, but I did have an ulterior motive. I wanted to find out if my hunch about James McGregor was correct. The last place I expected to get a lead on Alexander Skea was right next door, but I certainly wasn't going to turn it down.

EIGHTEEN

As we pushed away from the store on our bikes, Chase suggested heading south out of town. The hills are a little less brutal at that end of the county, and we could pick up a bike trail through the woods about three miles past the city limits.

I knew that Chase rode the tougher routes up into the mountains routinely, but let's just say that even though I'm in pretty good shape, I'm hardly training for the Tour de France. While I was upstairs, he'd switched his lean, mean road bike out for a more casual hybrid with suspension like my own ride that would handle the forest path.

We pedaled along companionably, waving at townsfolk out in their yards mowing the grass or just sitting in lawn chairs drinking sweet tea and passing the time of day. A couple of dogs trotted along after us in half-hearted pursuit, but neither one of them even bothered to bark.

Before we'd gone a mile, I was already reveling in that marvelous feeling of freedom that always comes over me on a bicycle. I love the smooth feel of pavement rolling under the wheels and the way the breeze from the forward motion picks up my hair and blows it back.

I know, I know. I'm supposed to be wearing a helmet, but what can I say? I ran with sparklers when I was kid

133

and drank out of the garden house. When you take those kinds of risks and live, you're a thrill seeker for life.

Chase and I had ridden together before and to our delight discovered we can strike a good matching pace. The first time we took the bikes out, I was ridiculously pleased when Chase said admiringly, "Hey! You can keep up!"

I know. It *could* have been a condescending comment. I guess you would have had to hear the inflection he put on the words to really understand that it wasn't. In the couple of months I'd been in Briar Hollow, I'd observed that while everyone knows Chase and he has some casual friends like my contractor, Mark Haskell, the guy is really kind of a loner.

When he said that about me being able to keep up, I instantly understood that Chase was pleased to have some-one to ride with, and I think a little extra pleased that that someone was me.

As we neared the outskirts of town, Chase told me about his week in the cobbler's shop and I talked about ordering the espresso machine and our plans for the coffee bar. By the time we turned into the forest, I felt energized and alive, enjoying the sights and sounds of nature around me.

At the 10-mile mark, Chase suggested we stop at an overlook on the trail right by a cascading waterfall. He reached in his saddlebags and brought out an apple, which he sliced with a folding knife, using the same implement to divide up a hunk of sharp cheddar cheese.

I wasn't expecting an impromptu picnic, but the instant I saw the food, my stomach growled. I hadn't had anything to eat since breakfast that morning.

"What were you all doing over at the library?" Chase asked, munching on an apple slice.

The cardinal rule of fabricated stories is don't mix it up too much.

"Tori is taking an online class," I said, faithfully sticking to the story du jour. "It's kind of a history, genealogy, ancestry *thing*. She was looking for some information on a guy from the Orkney Islands named Alexander Skea who settled around here back in the 1800s."

For just an instant, I thought Chase had heard the name before. An odd look came over his face when I said Alexander's name, but then Chase grimaced in annoyance and swatted at a fly buzzing around his head.

"I like everything about the outdoors except bugs," he grumbled. "Especially the ones trying to steal my food."

"Aw, come on now," I laughed, "we're the ones invading their territory."

"I cannot adopt a liberal position where insects are concerned," he said, slapping at the buzzing fly again.

When his personal air space was once again clear, Chase said, "So, did Tori find what she was looking for?"

"Yes and no," I answered. "She found a picture that she thinks has the guy in it."

"How does she know what he looked like?" Chase asked.

I walked right into that one, forcing myself to expand our fictional backstory a little bit.

"The picture kind of looks like one she saw online," I improvised.

"Really?" Chase said. "Where?"

"Oh, you know, one of those places where people make their family trees," I said vaguely.

Before he had a chance to ask me anything else, I added, "Want to see the picture?"

He looked at me suspiciously. "Am I going to have to report you to Linda for stealing things from the Historical Association?" he asked with a fake, disapproving glower.

Laughing, I said, "Of course not. I took a picture of the picture."

Which technically wasn't against the rules either, because I hadn't used the flash.

Digging my phone out of my pocket, I found the copy of the group photo and handed the device to Chase.

He looked at the screen with interest, and then observed ruefully, "They don't look like they were having much fun, do they?"

"I read somewhere that people had to sit still for a long time to have their picture taken back then," I replied. "It's why people in old photos always look so miserable."

"These guys sure qualify for that description," he agreed.

"I don't guess you recognize any of them, do you?" I asked, trying to sound casual.

"Hey!" Chase cried with mock outrage. "Just how *old* do you think I am, anyway?"

"I'm just giving you a hard time," I said. "And I'm not telling you the whole truth. See that guy there in the middle? The inscription penciled on the back of the photo says his name was James McGregor. I was wondering if he might be related to you."

Chase used his thumb and forefinger to enlarge the image, staring at it more closely. "Well, would you look at that," he said finally. "I think you might be right. My great-great-something grandfather *was* named James McGregor. I think my dad had a picture of him."

It suddenly dawned on me that although Chase and I had talked about a lot of things in our lives, including *my* family, he'd never had much to say about his own.

"I didn't realize your people were from around here," I said, probing gently for more information.

"My dad moved away from Briar Hollow when he was just a little kid," Chase said easily. "I was raised in Raleigh."

"Why did you move back?" I asked. "It had to be quite a change of pace for you."

Chase moved his hand in a sweeping gesture that took in the forest setting around us. "Look at this place," he said. "It's beautiful. Just because I was raised in the city doesn't mean I like it. Plus, I'd heard stories about Briar Hollow my whole life. I kind of thought of moving here as coming home."

That was easy enough to understand. Raleigh is a beautiful city, but there's still almost half a million people living there, which is around 498,000 too many for me.

"So I guess your great-great-granddaddy and this Alexander guy must have been Lodge brothers or something," I said.

"Or something," Chase agreed.

There was something funny about the way he spoke the words, but he didn't give me any time to think that through. Instead he said suddenly, as if just struck by the inspiration, "Hey, with all this talk about pictures, why don't we take one? Do you know how to use the timer on that thing?"

"I do," I said, "but couldn't we just take a selfie?"

"Nobody looks good in a selfie," he said. "Besides, let's try to get the waterfall in the picture. It'll be pretty."

He had a point about the selfies. That monkey who took a picture of himself looks better than I do even after fourteen tries.

Eyeing the clearing for something to set the phone on, I spotted a stump across from the bench we were sitting on. "Hold on."

Thankfully my iPhone case has a thick, flat edge so I knew the phone would sit upright and the stump was just high enough to help me frame the shot. When everything was set up, I hurried over and plopped down beside Chase.

"Okay," I said, "we don't have long, so smile."

Smiling turned out to be the easy part.

Chase immediately put his arm around me and drew me close. When the shutter clicked, our heads were almost touching and I was grinning from ear to ear.

Pretty much like that monkey that took a picture of himself.

Chase, however, seemed to approve of the photo wholeheartedly.

"Send me that, will you?" he said. "It's really good, especially with the waterfall behind us. You framed it perfectly."

Glancing at the signal indicator, I realized I had no bars. I promised I'd send him the picture when we were back in connected civilization, and then we went on with our bike ride. There was no more talk of Alexander Skea. By the time we got back to the shop, the light was failing. We said our goodnights and I wheeled my bike into the store. Tori heard me come in and called out from her apartment, "Hey, I'm back here! Come tell me about your ride."

Her door was open, sending a long rectangle of light slanting out across the store. It almost felt like I was following the yellow brick road, which was pretty funny because I found Tori and our resident munchkin sitting in front of her new flat screen eating popcorn.

"Hey, you two," I said, dropping down on the couch beside Darby. "What are you watching?"

"We just finished a moving picture about tall blue people who defend their tree against bad men," Darby answered.

Translation. *Avatar*.

"How was the bike ride?" Tori asked.

"Good," I replied. "We took the bike path down to the falls and back."

She let out a low whistle. "How far is that?"

"About twenty miles round trip," I said.

"You must have it *bad* for this guy," she said.

Tori is one of those lucky souls who can live on junk food and never gain an ounce. She claims she doesn't work out because of a rare allergy—to exercise equipment.

I shot her the "don't ask me about a guy in front of the children" look, which she understood instantly.

"Hey, Darb Man," she said smoothly, "how about giving us some girl time?"

The little brownie looked at her, then looked at me, and said placidly, "You want to talk about things you don't want me to hear."

And did I mention the "children" are perceptive?

"Yup," she said, "you nailed it."

Darby frowned, probably thinking about the phrase "nailed it," and then apparently deciding it meant he was right and no actual hammers were involved.

Once he had all that worked out, the little guy actually held out little arms and gave Tori a hug.

"Hey!" I protested. "What about me?"

Darby's whole face lit up and he more or less threw himself at me. I caught him and held him in a fierce bear hug. He was so happy he felt like a quivering puppy in my embrace.

When I let him go, he said simply, "I will be in the basement if you need me, Mistress Jinx." And just like that, he was gone.

"Is he not, hands down, the cutest thing you've ever seen?" Tori asked, smiling fondly.

"Pretty much," I agreed.

"Okay. So, now," she said, "how was the ride?"

"Great," I grinned. "You want to see the picture we took of ourselves?"

She let out a little squeal. "Yes!! You're taking pictures of yourselves. That is an *excellent* sign!"

I rolled my eyes as I handed her the phone. She looked at the screen and then her smile wilted a little at the edges.

She enlarged part of the photo, looked again . . . and still said *nothing*. Great. Did I have a zit on my nose I'd missed or something?

Finally, I couldn't stand it any longer.

"*What?*" I demanded.

Tori gave me the phone back. She'd blown up a section of the spray coming off the waterfall. Alexander Skea's face was staring out at me.   .

When I could speak again, I said, "That's impossible. Didn't you tell me that people think they see faces in photos all the time and it's called matri-something?"

"Matrixing," she replied. "But it's kind of different when you can actually *recognize* the face, Jinksy."

"I don't buy it," I said stubbornly.

"You don't *want* to buy it," she countered. "And besides, it's easy enough to prove. Email me that photo and the close-up you took of Skea's face from the group shot."

I did as I was told and watched as Tori opened her MacBook, downloaded both photos from the email, and spent a few minutes clicking keys. When she turned the laptop toward me, she'd created a side-by-side comparison.

Alexander's face from the group photo was on the left, and the misty face from my picture at the waterfall was on the right. There was no point arguing any more. It was the same man.

"I thought you didn't see anything about Skea when you held the picture," Tori said.

"I didn't," I protested. "But I did feel a kind of . . . I don't know . . . *tingling* sensation, maybe?"

"Maybe what you felt was him," she said, pointing at the screen.

"So he what, followed me on a bike ride to try to get my attention?" I asked.

"Sort of looks like it, doesn't it?" Tori said.

"Why doesn't he just show up like all the other ghosts do?"

It's not like I'd ever had any trouble talking to dead folks before. Just the opposite, in fact. They usually show up when I don't want them to.

"Maybe he can't," Tori suggested.

"How are we supposed to figure that out?"

We stared at each other for a second, and then said in unison, "Darby."

NINETEEN

We hadn't taken three steps down toward the basement before the fruits of Darby's labor became apparent. Literally. What had been a dank, musty black hole was now a brightly lit cavern that smelled distinctly of lemons and fresh oranges.

Either the little guy really liked his cleaning products, or I had a citrus grove under the store. The way my life was going? I'd have laid even odds on either one.

Then we heard the music.

Abba. *Dancing Queen*.

I turned toward Tori. "*Seriously*?" I asked.

She shrugged helplessly. "We watched *Mama Mia,* and he realized he missed the Seventies."

As I looked out over the now immaculate, well-lit basement, I was suddenly struck by how big it was. Like *too* big. I couldn't see any of the other walls, just newly installed shelves. Rows and rows of them that stretched out in all directions holding neatly labeled bins and boxes of all sizes and shapes. To tell you the truth? It looked a lot like the set of *Warehouse 13*.

"Is it just my imagination," I asked, "or does the basement seem a lot *bigger* than the store itself?"

"Aunt Fiona did say the store is built on a fairy mound," Tori said. "Maybe this is it?"

"Uh, okay, but what the heck *is* all this stuff?"

From the bottom of the stairs, Darby spoke up. "Mistress Jinx," he said reproachfully, "I was not ready for you to see this yet. It is not well organized."

Because in his version of English "organized" has another definition?

"Sorry, Darby," I said, slowly starting down the stairs again. "We just wanted to talk to you about something. I didn't realize what you've been doing down here was meant to be a surprise. This place looks amazing. And *big*. Like really, *really* big. Uh, how big, exactly?"

"As big as is required," he said cryptically.

I decided I didn't want to know.

"What *is* all this?" I asked, waving my arm toward the shelves.

"Things you might need," he replied.

Well, yeah, if I was planning to be the star of the new reality series, *Hoarders: The Reformed Ones*.

Before I could figure out how to reframe my question and possibly get a better answer, I heard Tori gasp.

"Jinksy," she said, breathless with excitement, "we have a *lair*."

Did I want a lair?

Following her gaze, I saw that the area under the stairs was essentially a three-sided room—with a fireplace, no less, flanked by floor-to-ceiling book cases. Darby had paneled the walls in rich, burled wood that matched the planking on the floor—at least in the spots that weren't covered with plush Oriental rugs.

Leather furniture was arranged around a medium-height, heavy oak table that was obviously meant to be a work space. One corner was completely dominated by a massive roll top desk, which was closed at the moment.

Tori, who was even more book-obsessed than I am, made a beeline for the first set of shelves. She took down a volume bound in rich, red leather and opened it to look at the first page.

"Oh. My. God," she said. "Jinx, you need to come look at this."

The fact that she didn't use her habitual nickname for me clued me in that she had found something major.

When I joined her, she handed me the book. The yellowed pages felt thick and supple in my hands. The flyleaf was inscribed in a flowing script laid down with an old-fashioned fountain pen.

I squinted and looked closer.

Scratch that.

With a quill.

Unsure I was actually reading the words correctly, I spoke them aloud, "The Grimoire of Martha Hamilton, *caute intrant.*"

I looked up. "What the heck does that mean?"

"Enter with caution," Darby said from behind me.

I hastily, and *very* carefully, re-shelved the book.

"Okay, Darby," I said. "Talk."

"Before Mistress Fiona left," he said, "she told me that all of the records and materials that belonged to the coven were hidden here in the basement. She confessed to having allowed them to fall into some disorder. She thought it might be helpful to you if I organized this space and made it a place where you can further your studies."

He fidgeted a little, and then added, "She said it was not working out well for you to get your magical information from the Internet."

Okay, make that two t-shirts reading, "Got understatement?"

"Do you mean to tell me that all of this time I have been sitting on a whole basement, magic cave, reference library *place*?" I said indignantly. "Don't you think it might have been good for me to *know* that?"

Tori chimed in. "I think it's more like a magical Super Walmart without the Walmartians," she suggested.

"You're *not* helping, Tori," I snapped.

And besides, how did she know the Walmartians weren't down here?

"With all respect, Mistress," Darby said, standing his ground, "knowing what was here would have done you no good. You would not have been able to locate anything useful."

"He's quite correct," a female voice said. "You weren't ready for any of this."

Tori and I both whirled around to find an older woman walking toward us out of the stacks. She was dressed in black pants and wore a heavy, gray cardigan over a simple white blouse. Her hair was pulled up in a bun held in place with a yellow, No. 2 pencil; a look perfectly complemented by the round, black glasses perched on her nose.

Suddenly, I knew exactly who she was.

"Myrtle?" I asked.

"Hi," she said simply, smiling at us warmly.

"You're *human*?" Tori said.

"No," Myrtle replied, gesturing for us to sit down. Which was good, because we were probably in danger of falling down.

"You need me to appear human," she continued, when we were seated. "I picked a persona that seemed to match my surroundings and your perception of what I *should* look like. Fiona, in her usual fashion, is being a bit disorderly disseminating useful information. Which I realize is another of the many understatements currently plaguing your existence, Jinx."

"Oh, great," I groaned. "You're a mind reader, too."

She laughed, and I recognized the sound; it was her usual three-note trill, but more lyrically augmented.

"No," Myrtle said, "the privacy of your thoughts is

undisturbed, but since I *am* the store, I am afforded a unique vantage point. Let's just say I pick up on things."

I had chosen one of the leather chairs by the fireplace, which we actually needed as a source of warmth because the basement was several degrees cooler than the upstairs. Tori was across from me, and Myrtle faced the fire so we formed a kind of loose circle.

"Can I ask some questions?" I said.

"Of course," Myrtle said, "that's what I'm here for."

"Are you a fairy?"

"No," she said. "I am the magic that animates this place. In my natural state, I have no physical form. Think of me as a kind of guiding energy."

"That sort of makes you sound . . . uh . . . godlike," Tori ventured uncertainly.

"Hardly," Myrtle said. "There is only One, great, organizing Intelligence in creation that we all revere by different names. I am not that One. Given the way Jinx was thrust into the middle of all these affairs, and the jumbled manner in which she has been receiving guidance, I simply felt it was time for me to lend a more *solid* hand. Does that make sense?"

Tori frowned. "So, uh, you're going to be Alfred to Jinksy's Batman?" she asked.

Myrtle smiled. "More like Giles to her Buffy."

Oh. God. Don't tell me . . .

On that point, Myrtle did seem to read my mind.

"Without the vampires," she added. "Those don't actually exist. At least not the ones that feed on human blood."

I blew out the breath I didn't realize I'd been holding. Oh thank . . .

Huh?

There are other kinds of . . .

I stopped that train of thought before it ever left the station. If I wouldn't have looked ridiculous, I'd have put my fingers in my ears and starting chanting, "la, la, la,la,la, la, la."

Stay in the moment, Jinx.

"But what if someone finds you here?" I asked. "How am I supposed to explain you?"

"Don't worry about that," Myrtle assured me. "If anyone else opens the door and looks down here, they will see nothing but a musty basement full of useless junk."

Then, assuming a businesslike air, she said, "Now, I believe you came down here to ask about the ghostly image of Alexander Skea in the photo you took today?"

Finally. Somebody who didn't need *CliffsNotes*.

"Was that really his ghost in the mist behind us?" I asked.

"I believe it was," Myrtle said. "Can you please show the photo to Darby?"

When I held the phone out to Darby, he nodded his head vigorously. "Yes, that is my Master."

"Do you know why he would try to make his presence known like this?" Myrtle asked.

To my surprise, Darby touched the screen with his tiny fingers and enlarged the image to show the whole scene. The little guy catches on fast.

"Oh, yes," he said. "The waterfall was a special place for Mistress Knasgowa."

"I thought that might be the case," Myrtle said. "Waterfalls and wells are often gateways to other dimensions."

"So, you think Alexander is trying to find Knasgowa?" I asked.

"Possibly," Myrtle said.

"Then why can't I talk to him the way I talk to Beau and the other spirits?"

"I cannot be certain," Myrtle said, "but I think Knasgowas must have placed a spell on Alexander, so that when he died, his spirit would be unable to manifest in this realm. They were, after all, concerned about two things; keeping Brenna Sinclair trapped in limbo and preventing her from finding Alexander if she did escape."

"But he's dead," I said. "What could Brenna want with whatever is left of his body?"

The minute I said it, I regretted asking the question because I knew I wasn't going to like the answer.

Color me right.

"If Brenna can find Alexander's remains," Myrtle said, "she can grind his bones into a powder and use it to cast a locator spell. She will be able to find every single living person who carries a drop of Alexander's blood, and by extension, her own."

"And then what?" Tori asked.

"As Fiona explained, some of Alexander's descendants will have more power than others," Myrtle said. "Brenna could use magic to influence matings that would, over time, strengthen her bloodline. Power is an intoxicating lure. She would surely be able to convince some of Alexander's descendants to embrace their heritage and become her followers. Remember, she is immortal. She can afford to be patient."

Influence *matings*?

I guess I should have already put that one together, but it still seriously freaked me out.

"So," I said slowly, "we need to locate Alexander's body in order to find his journal so we can put Brenna back where she belongs, but we can't let Brenna find Alexander because she'll put operation Magic Baby Daddy in motion."

The corner of Myrtle's mouth crooked into a smile. "That's a rather droll way to put all the pieces together, but, yes, you are correct."

"Okay. So, one way or the other, I *do* need to talk to Alexander Skea," I said. "How do we make that happen?"

"If you can get his spirit here in the store," Myrtle said,

"his proximity to me will have the same effect it has on Colonel Longworth and Fiona. Alexander will become stable enough to speak and interact with you."

"How do we get him to come here?" I asked.

Darby supplied the answer. "My Master will only come if Mistress Knasgowa tells him to," the brownie said. "He will trust no other."

Something told me we were headed into the woods.

TWENTY

The first ghost stories began to circulate around town that Monday morning. I ran down to George and Irma's grocery store on the corner bright and early to pick up some doughnuts and found a knot of people clustered around the security camera monitor by the cash register.

The bell on the front door jingled when I came in, so Irma spotted me immediately. "Jinx!" she cried. "You have to come see what the store camera caught last night!"

Two or three people made room for me as I wedged into the little group. Irma rewound the video, which at first showed nothing but an overhead angle of the empty store. Then, I saw a box of Twinkies levitate off the shelf and float serenely toward the cash register.

As we watched, the box settled on the countertop. There was a kind of vague flickering on the screen in a size and shape that could have been a person, and then the image settled back on the empty store.

"Can you *believe* that?" Irma said. "It looks for all the world like that ghost tried to *pay* for those Twinkies. I found the box sitting right here when I opened up this morning."

"Wow!" I said, feigning the required astonishment. "How did you know to look at the recording?"

A sick feeling had begun to settle in the pit of my stomach. This could only mean one thing. We were running out of time to get those spirits back where they belonged before Briar Hollow became paranormal ground zero.

"The system's got a motion sensor, honey," Irma said. "You really ought to have one put in your store, too. The little light was flashing, so I checked the footage from last night. We had a big ole raccoon breaking in here last year stealing food. We like to have *never* caught the varmint. I figured the blinking was about something like that. I never expected to see flying Twinkies."

Well, I mean really, who *does*?

Before I could come up with an answer I could actually say out loud, several people started talking at once. It seemed that over the weekend there had been a number of strange sightings around town. None of those episodes had been quite this dramatic, although one woman did summon the Sheriff when she was positive she saw her dead husband trying to unlock the front door to their house.

I filled up a white sack with doughnuts and paid for them, leaving the crowd to watch the flying Twinkies again. Thankfully my shop was empty when I got back and Darby had the coffee ready. As I was telling Tori what I had just seen, Beau materialized in the doorway and walked into the storeroom.

"That is what I came to tell you," he said, overhearing the last of my account. "It has started. The newly risen spirits are beginning to become highly frustrated. The discontent is fueling their energy and their abilities. My associates and I spent most of last night trying to maintain order, but I fear there will be more of these incidents."

So that's why we hadn't seen him yesterday.

After we filled the Colonel in on the most recent developments in our research, he asked to see the photograph of the Masonic officers. I thought Beau was interested in Alexander Skea, but it was the name "James McGregor" that had caught his attention.

"That is him," Beau said, pointing to the central figure in the group. "It was James McGregor who found me on the battlefield. He searched my body for identification and found this."

Beau removed the heavy pocketwatch from the vest of his uniform and opened the case. Inside, the engraving read, "To Brother Beauregard T. Longworth, Master Mason, with gratitude for his service. Harmony Lodge No. 1."

"You were a Mason?" I asked.

"I *am* a Mason," Beau corrected me. "I was raised in the same Lodge where Brother Andrew Jackson took his first degree in 1805. My father was among the officers at his initiation."

"So James McGregor saw your watch and knew you were a Mason?" I asked.

"Yes," Beau said. "The local Lodge buried me with full Masonic rites. I am deeply indebted to this man. He went to great lengths to not only arrange my funeral, but also to contact my wife. If Brother Skea was a member of the same Lodge, I have no doubt he was also a good man, and is, insofar as he is now able, attempting to help you."

There was only one way I knew to reach across my side of that void and boost Alexander's "signal." I had to go back out to the waterfall and try to reach Knasgowa, especially since Myrtle and Darby were absolutely certain Alexander wouldn't—and possibly couldn't—show up without the okay from his wife.

Tori had been completely on board with the whole plan until Myrtle suggested I attempt contact at midnight, an hour when she said the boundary "between realms" was thinner.

"Whoa, whoa, whoa," Tori protested. "Midnight is, like, after dark."

"Generally," I observed mildly.

"The last time we went skulking around outside in the

middle of the night a crazy dude with a tomahawk tried to kill us," she said.

"Tori, I'm pretty sure that was a one-time thing," I said. "And besides, you don't have to come."

I knew that suggestion would shut her up pretty fast.

Well. Okay. Not shut her up, but at least change the tone of the grumbling.

Right on cue Tori shot me a wounded look.

"Don't be ridiculous," she said. "I wouldn't send you out there to be eaten by bears without a witness to report the location of whatever is left of your body."

Oh, crud. I hadn't thought about bears.

Tori looked triumphant. "Gotcha," she said, grinning.

Which she had. Not that we were keeping score or anything.

Tori was watching the conflicting thoughts playing out on my face.

"Of course I'm going with you," she said, more seriously, "just don't ask me to like it. And don't try to convince me you're thrilled about the whole 'back to nature in the dead of night' thing either."

She just had to use the word "dead," didn't she?

I couldn't dispute the fact that neither one of us has ever been described as "outdoorsy." At least we weren't going to hike to the waterfall. That would have meant a five-mile walk through the woods. Tori was heading out to WallyWorld after lunch to buy a bike and stick a headlight on it. We'd drive to the trailhead and start riding in around 11 o'clock that night.

When we ran this all down for Beau, he said, "I am coming with you."

"Don't you think you better stay in town and try to keep the peace?" I asked.

He shook his head. "Alexander Skea and I are from a similar time and we are Masonic brothers. If he is reluctant to materialize, I may be able to communicate with him in ways that you cannot."

That was actually a good point.

Darby had wanted to come along, too, but when he mentioned it the night before, Myrtle gently told him she needed him to stay with her. The little brownie held her in such high esteem that he didn't protest. He just bowed his head and said, "As you wish, Your Majesty."

A few minutes later, after Darby went upstairs to make a pot of tea, I asked Myrtle why she didn't want Darby going along with us to the falls.

"Like all brownies, Darby has the heart of a lion," Myrtle said, smiling, "but it is encased in the body of a child."

Tori and I had exchanged a look. "Are you saying it's going to be dangerous out there?" she asked.

"I'm saying there's no need to put the smallest of us in Brenna Sinclair's way," Myrtle said. "Especially when we have no idea where she is or what she's doing."

Since Darby was once again hard at work in the basement, I shared that conversation with Beau as well, expressing my reservations about *his* welfare.

The old soldier looked amused. "I appreciate your concern, Miss Jinx, but as I am already dead, what do you think this sorceress can do to me?"

"I honestly don't know," I said earnestly, "I just know I don't want her doing it."

Beau reached out and patted the back of my hand. The impact of his fingers was cool and whisper light.

"I assure you that I will be fine, my dear," he said. "I am quite capable of taking care of myself."

It took all I had not to ask if he could take care of us, too. I knew that once Beau was outside the walls of the store, he was completely noncorporeal. It would have been wrong of me to make him feel responsible for looking after me and Tori. But truthfully? The sun was still up, our excursion was at least 12 hours away, and I was already scared to death.

The rest of the day passed far too quickly for my tastes. Why is it that when you *want* time to crawl it whizzes past at hyperspeed?

When we couldn't put off our departure any longer, we quietly loaded the bikes in my Prius and silently glided the hybrid out of the alley behind the store. The lights were on next door in Chase's apartment and at Amity Prescott's, but no curious faces appeared in either set of windows.

I did, however, almost have a heart attack when I looked in the rearview mirror and saw Beau sitting in the backseat.

"*Geez!*" I yelped. "Beau! What's with the stealth mode?"

"My apologies," he said, dipping his head in a little bow. "I only just this moment appeared."

"Well, ring a bell or something next time," I said. "You scared me half to death."

The old soldier regarded me with a bemused expression. "You do seem somewhat discomfited this evening."

Discomfited?

Okay, now he was just messing with me.

We didn't say much on the drive out to the trailhead, although Tori did yelp a couple of times when I swerved to miss hitting wandering spirits.

"Jinksy!" she cried the third time. "They're *dead*. As in not living. You don't have to avoid hitting them."

"How would you like to be dead and have a cherry red Prius go barreling right through the middle of you?" I demanded.

I don't know. It just seems wrong to run over people even if they are already, well, roadkill.

A slight chuckle emanated from the backseat. I glanced into the rearview mirror and said with annoyance, "You're certainly in a good mood tonight."

Beau arranged his features in a more dignified expression, but his eyes twinkled. "I have always quite enjoyed late night reconnaissance work."

Terrific. I had the Confederate version of Rambo in the backseat.

When we reached the parking lot at the trailhead, the only things that jumped out at us were the posted signs saying no one is supposed to be in there after dark. Thankfully, there's a little Prius-size clearing to one side as well. I carefully pulled the car into the cover of the trees and we got out.

While Beau watched, Tori and I hosed each other down with Deep Woods Off.

"That substance repels insects?" he asked with interest.

"It does," I said. "There are mosquitos in there big enough to pick you up and carry you off."

He shook his head. "We certainly could have used *that* modern marvel in my day."

Tori hadn't even been on her bike yet, so I instructed her to pedal a couple of loops around the lot. After adjusting the height of the seat and the angle of the handlebars, she was much steadier in the saddle. I was also pleased to discover that the combined beams of our headlights gave us more than enough illumination to navigate the smooth, paved trail safely.

We stood astride our bikes looking down the dark tunnel into the trees. Around us the woods were alive with night sounds.

"This isn't going to get any easier," I said. "We might as well go in there."

Tori gulped. "To find the ghost of a Cherokee witch so she can tell her dead husband to materialize for us and dish on how to stick a Scottish bitch back in the bottle."

"That's pretty much it," I said.

"But there's no tomahawks this time, right?" she persisted.

"Not that I'm aware of," I said. Turning to Beau, I asked, "Are you ready?"

He levitated a few inches off the ground. "Fear not," he replied. "I will keep up."

"Then we're good to go," I said. "Tori?"

"Yep," she said, standing up and putting her weight into the first pedal stroke. "Off to see the wizard."

Crap.

Just what I *didn't* need to be thinking about at that moment.

Flying monkeys.

TWENTY-ONE

Weird shadows played across the trail as we pedaled into the forest. I caught the occasional glimpse of laser eyes in the darkness, assuring myself that none of them looked big enough to belong to an animal capable of eating us.

Then I remembered that beady little eyes are supposed to be a criminal trait.

But a bear isn't a criminal, right?

He's just out there in the woods being a bear . . . and I was more or less trespassing in his dining room.

Which made *me* the criminal.

Yes, that is actually how my mind works.

When I'm nervous—or scared half to death—I engage in mental babble.

Okay. Now, stop.

I did *not* just tell you that I listen to the voices.

Because there are no voices.

Not exactly, anyway.

There are multiple trains of thought up here in my noggin going on all the time. That night one of the trains was the What the *Hell* Are You Doing Express, set to arrive at Platform Midnight.

Moving stuff with my mind?

Convenient.

Getting visions from objects?

Cool.

Talking to ghosts?

Fun.

And then somebody just *had* to go throw a resurrected sorceress into the room and ruin the party.

Oh. Wait.

That was *me*.

Part of *me* wanted to go to the waterfall and meet Knasgowa. After all, I am her great-great-something-granddaughter.

But another part of me wanted to go back to who I was before Aunt Fiona died and I found out there was *so* much more to the world than I ever realized.

Tori, who was riding to my left, suddenly said, "Knock it off, Jinksy."

"Knock what off?" I asked, keeping my eyes on the trail.

"You're thinking so loud I can hear you all the way over here," she said. "Don't sweat it. We've got this."

"Where's all this bravery coming from?" I asked, giving her a quick glance and catching sight of her grin in the darkness.

"Fake it 'til you make it, kiddo," she said. "This is me. Faking it and not falling off this bike all at the same time."

I instantly picked up the beat.

"I'm a bigger faker than you are," I said, tauntingly.

"Are not."

"Am, too."

Ridiculously silly, and so, *so* comforting.

After that, I stopped worrying about the laser eyes and concentrated on getting where we were going.

A few minutes later we glided to a stop in the clearing. It was about a quarter of midnight. Darby told us that Knasgowa liked to sit in a cluster of boulders on the shore directly across from the waterfall. Even a couple of hundred years later, there was only one spot that matched his description.

The plan was for Tori and Beau to keep watch from the overlook while I climbed down to the rocks by myself. The surface of the pond rippled gently in the moonlight, moving outward from the cascading water. A kind of peace descended around me as I watched the undulating reflections. Suddenly, I was no longer afraid.

Getting down the slope was a lot easier than I anticipated, and so was finding Knasgowa. She was just sitting there on a low, flat boulder waiting for me. I glanced back up at Tori and Beau, but they were talking quietly and didn't seem to notice anything unusual.

"They cannot see me, granddaughter," Knasgowa said. "This time is for us alone. Come sit with me."

I don't know what I expected her to look like. Pocahontas from the Disney movie maybe?

Knasgowa could have been any age. She was dressed in simple blue gingham, with her long, black hair parted in the middle, pulled back, and done up in a bun. Had it not been for the rich, brown tone of her skin, the Cherokee woman would have passed for any pioneer wife straight out of the history books.

"Uh, hi," I said, easing myself down onto a boulder across from her. "I'm Jinx."

She smiled at me and that's when her magic touched me for the first time. The sensation was familiar; the same, kindness and warmth that had radiated from Aunt Fiona in life.

"You don't like your real name, do you?" Knasgowa asked, the corners of her eyes crinkling with mirth.

"I'm named after a movie star . . ."

The sentence stuttered to a stop. Did Knasgowa know anything about our world?

She laughed at my confusion; a liquid, lyrical sound

that made me think of butterflies dancing in a summer meadow.

"I know what a movie star is," she said. "On this side all is . . . joined. We are more than the sum of our time and our personal experiences. What I understand is no longer tied to my tribe or the number of the year in which I lived or died. Those things are just human devices to create order and make sense of the world. There's more to it than all that, which is what scares you so much, isn't it, Jinx?"

Before I had time to think, I blurted, "It's all too big for me."

Knasgowa patted the rock beside her. "Come sit with me, granddaughter. I will not harm you."

Harm me? I wanted to crawl up in her lap like a little kid.

When I moved closer to her, Knasgowa caught hold of my hand. Her fingers were strong and warm, nothing like Colonel Longworth's spectral touch.

"What are you?" I asked.

"I am myself," she said, "and to you I am your grandmother and your guide. I hope we will have many talks in this place. Don't be afraid of the woods at night. The animals can sense your magic just as the hickory tree did the night you spoke with it of the time before there was time."

"You know about that?" I asked. "How?"

"I am your ancestor," she said. "All who came before you watch over you, Jinx. You are never alone. Just because Fiona is joyful and pretends to meander in her course, do not think that she will not use her power to protect you if the need arises."

"Protect me?" I said. "She won't even give me a straight answer."

Knasgowa laughed again. "There are some things you must learn on your own to fully awaken your powers.

Fiona has never told you an untruth, she's just left a few things out."

I looked down at our joined hands and spoke softly. "I'm sorry I turned Brenna loose."

"It wasn't your fault," Knasgowa said. "When I consigned Brenna Sinclair to limbo at the moment of my passing, I knew she would not be held there forever. Her ambitious hunger for power is too strong."

"What do I do, grandmother?" which seemed like the most natural thing in the world to call this woman.

"When I leave you tonight, dig a little ways under this rock and you will find a silver cup given to me by Alexander on the day of our marriage," she said. "He brought it with him from Scotland. Return to the one you call Myrtle and she will help you to use the cup to summon my husband's spirit."

"But isn't he here with you?" I asked.

My question sent a kind of lonely sadness over her features. "No," she said. "We cannot be together in this place. Alexander dare not emerge from his own sort of limbo unless he is in a protected place. Brenna will sense his spirit and use her magic to find his grave. He can only pass into this realm in the cavern under your home. Brenna will not be able to sense him so long as he is with Myrtle."

She paused and then said softly, "When you speak with him, tell him I love him."

"I will," I said, the words barely passing over the lump in my throat. "Isn't there some way for the two of you to be together again?"

"That is not important right now," Knasgowa said. "Take the cup to Myrtle and do as she says. When you find the book that was buried with Alexander, use it to return those who have been awakened to their rightful slumber."

"And put Brenna back in limbo, right?" I asked.

Knasgowa shook her head. "I truly do not know if that

is possible," she said, "but you may be able to rob her of her immortality. Then you will have a . . ."

"Fair fight," I finished.

"Yes," she said. "But Brenna will still have her magic. She is determined to found her own hereditary line."

"But why?" I said. "I don't understand."

"There is much you do not yet understand and much you have to learn," Knasgowa said, "but each piece of that puzzle will come to you in its own time. I must go now. Take the cup to Myrtle and trust her to help you."

My fingers tightened on hers. "Please don't go," I pleaded. "There's so much I want to ask you."

Knasgowa leaned toward me and kissed me on the forehead. "Come here on nights like this when the moon is full and call to me. I will come to you and we will speak of many things. I love you, granddaughter."

A blanket of warmth settled around me, and she was gone. I wiped away the tears I hadn't even realized were rolling down my cheeks and called to Tori to join me. I heard her scramble down the slope, and then she and Colonel Longworth were with me among the boulders.

"Jinksy," Tori said, dropping to her knees in front of me and catching my hand, "you're crying. What happened?"

Looking down at her with shining eyes, I said, "She was here, Tori. Knasgowa was here. She's so beautiful and kind. I know you couldn't see her, but she was here. Honest."

Tori never hesitated. "I believe you, Jinksy," she said. "What did she tell you?"

The question snapped me back to reality. "Oh! We have to dig under this rock and find a cup that Alexander gave to her."

"Dig with what?" Tori asked. "We don't have a shovel."

Beau went down on one knee and examined the dirt

he couldn't actually touch. "The soil appears to be soft here," he said. "I don't think you'll need a shovel, and I may be able to be of some assistance in this regard."

"How?" I asked.

"There are some advantages to being insubstantial," he said.

We watched as he plunged his hand into the dirt at the base of the rock and began to move methodically around the edge. About halfway behind where I was sitting, he stopped, a thoughtful expression on his pale face.

"I believe the object you are searching for is here," he said, withdrawing his arm and indicating a spot on his sleeve just below the elbow. "At a depth of roughly this distance."

"And you couldn't just pull it out?" Tori asked.

Beau laughed. "Alas, no, Miss Tori," he said. "I can only detect subtle changes in the material through which my essence passes. If I were to hazard a guess, I would say the metal from which the cup is fashioned is silver?"

"Yes," I said, "that's what Knasgowa told me. How did you know?"

"Perhaps the metaphysical legends long associated with silver are correct," Beau said. "I can only tell you that when my hand passed through the space there in the ground I knew I was touching silver."

Interesting. We needed to run that one by Myrtle, too.

Tori and I found a couple of thick sticks lying at the edge of the pond and began to scrape away the soft dirt, following Beau's directions. Thanks to the moonlight and Beau's own faintly glowing form, we had enough light to see what we were doing.

His depth estimate seemed to be off, however. We kept digging, but we weren't finding anything. Then, about two feet down, the edge of the boulder appeared and the reason for the discrepancy became apparent.

"Reach up under the rock," Beau said. "I think the cup is secreted in a sort of hollowed out place in the stone."

Trying not to think about anything else that might be living under the rock, I put my hand inside the boulder and drew out a shallow, tarnished silver cup with a broad, flat handle on either side.

I have to tell you, I felt like we'd just stepped into an Indiana Jones movie.

"Holy crud," Tori said, "would you look at that!"

"Come on," I said. "We need to get this back to Myrtle."

We started to leave, but Beau stopped us. "Fill in the hole," he said, "and use a branch to rake the surface to appear more natural. I do not think it wise to leave behind evidence of this night's activities."

Incredibly good point.

When we climbed back up to the clearing, I carefully tucked the cup into the saddlebag on my bike. I turned toward the path and flicked on the headlight. That's when I saw the mountain lion.

Beside me, I heard Tori mutter something profane.

"Be still," Beau said. "Do not make any sudden movements and do not look into its eyes."

I'd like to tell you I did as I was told, but I couldn't have looked away from those eyes if I'd tried. They held me mesmerized, not just by the intensity in their deep, amber depths, but by their oddly familiar expression. I know it sounds ridiculous, but I swear to you I felt like I knew those eyes.

The encounter only lasted a few seconds before the big cat melted into the darkness, but the brief communication we shared felt far more timeless.

"Is it gone?" Tori whispered.

"Yes," I said calmly. "We can go now."

Beau frowned. "Miss Jinx," he said, "do you not think it would be more prudent to wait a few minutes?"

"No," I said, climbing on my bike. "Even if he's still here, he won't hurt us."

"Since when are you the mountain lion whisperer?" Tori hissed.

I couldn't answer her question then and I can't explain it to you now. Maybe it was just because Knasgowa had said I was safe in the woods. But I not only knew that big cat wouldn't hurt me, I knew that if I needed him to, he'd protect me.

TWENTY-TWO

Chase McGregor walked out of the maze of shelves in the basement and sat down across from Myrtle in the newly created area Tori had christened the "lair." He looked at Myrtle appraisingly. "For a minute there, I didn't think you were going to get Jinx to call it a night and go to bed," he said.

Myrtle removed her eyeglasses and pinched the bridge of her nose. Chase knew she didn't need the glasses to see, but the action fit her new human persona and seemed perfectly natural.

"I was telling her the truth," Myrtle said, settling the glasses once again on her face. "It *is* almost dawn, and that's the wrong time to use the quaich to summon the spirit of Alexander Skea."

Chase looked at the silver cup sitting on the table in front of her.

"May I?" he asked.

Myrtle nodded.

He reached for the cup, lifting it carefully, and turning it over in his hands. "I don't care if my name is McGregor," he said, sounding amused, "I still don't know how you get 'quake' out of q-u-a-i-c-h."

"There are more incomprehensible languages than Gaelic," Myrtle smiled, glancing back in the direction from which Chase had appeared. "Where is your father?"

On cue, a lame ginger cat trotted into the room on three legs and sat down in front of the fireplace, regarding them both with impassive green eyes.

Myrtle arched an eyebrow in his direction.

"Really, Festus," she said disapprovingly, "is it out of the question for you to be polite enough to appear in human form and sit down with us for a civil conversation?"

"Don't be putting on airs with me just because you've decided to become the head librarian around here, Myrtle," the cat grumbled. "I've explained this to you before. It's easier to limp on three legs than two."

Chase rolled his eyes. "Would the two of you just give it a rest?"

"If I were you," Myrtle said, turning her attention sharply back to him, "I wouldn't be attempting to lecture other people about their behavior. Exactly what were you thinking following Jinx out to the waterfall tonight?"

Chase shifted uncomfortably in his chair and stared down at the toes of his black boots. "She doesn't know it was me," he said. "She just thinks she had a close encounter with a *very* big kitty cat."

"A kitty cat whose *eyes* looked familiar to her," Myrtle said curtly.

Setting his jaw, Chase said stubbornly, "It is my job to protect her."

Festus stretched luxuriantly in the heat from the fireplace, circling until he found the perfect spot to lie down. Once he was arranged, the cat crossed his front paws and studied his son.

"Try selling that story to someone who's interested in buying it, " Festus said with pointed skepticism.

"What's that supposed to mean?" Chase protested, a faint red blush creeping across his tanned cheeks.

"It means you have feelings for the young woman,"

Myrtle said, delivering her words with more kindness than the acerbic tomcat. "You must be careful, Chase," she warned. "Falling in love with Jinx could cloud your judgment."

Chase sighed and looked up. "It's too late, Myrtle," he said softly. "I'm already in love with her."

Festus picked up one front paw, licked the fur, and scrubbed at his whiskers. "I told you so," he said, as he inclined his head to one side and rubbed behind his ear. "Now we're in for it."

Myrtle shook her head as she watched the cat with thinly disguised disapproval.

"I trust there will be no fleas in that carpet when you are done, Festus," she said in a prickly tone.

The cat stopped, paw in mid-air, his eyes widening with indignation. "Did you really just accuse me of having fleas?"

"*Enough!*" Chase said, smothering a smile. "Let's just stay on track here."

"Fine," Myrtle conceded, "but you're not going to like what I have to say."

"I know what you're going to say," Chase replied miserably. "I have to tell Jinx the truth about myself."

"Correct," Myrtle said. "She has to know about Clan McGregor eventually, but this budding relationship between the two of you somewhat complicates things. You cannot wait to tell her the truth."

Chase rubbed his eyes with one hand. "I don't suppose when you and Darby set this place up you remembered the Scotch?" he asked wearily.

"In the cabinet by the desk," Myrtle said.

Chase got up and crossed the expanse of Oriental rugs, letting out a low whistle of appreciation when he opened the cabinet. "Is there a make of single malt you don't have in here?" he asked.

"Of course not," she said, sounding mildly offended. "The Oban is on the top shelf."

"Dad, do you want some?" Chase asked, taking down a tall bottle of amber liquid.

"What a silly question," the cat said archly. "Of course I do."

Chase poured himself a glass of whisky, filling a jigger for Festus, which he sat down on the hearth. The old cat dipped his tongue appreciatively in the liquor, purring loudly.

"Better than mother's milk," he said appreciatively, licking his whiskers.

Reclaiming his chair, Chase said, "Look, Myrtle, I really think Jinx has been hit with too much already. She really doesn't need to know about our kind just yet."

Festus brought his head up from his drink abruptly.

"I don't like your tone, boy," he said. "You make it sound like being a werecat is a bad thing. We are an old and proud race, royal in our own right. The McGregors have protected Knasgowa's line since the 18th century."

"I don't need a history lesson," Chase said. "It's just that all the other witches in the family were prepared from childhood to understand our world. Jinx knows nothing, and this is all coming at her too fast."

"It's hardly our fault that Jinx's mother turned her back on her own heritage," Myrtle said. "Fiona tried to influence the child. Kelly wouldn't allow it."

Chase shook his head. "Let's just get everything settled back down again and then I'll tell her," he said. "It's not information she needs right now. Knowing about me won't help to control Brenna Sinclair or give the restless spirits peace."

Without warning, Fiona appeared in the chair across from him. She looked Myrtle up and down and said, "Good heavens, didn't you go just a bit severe with the look?"

Myrtle regarded the other woman over the top of her glasses. "Aren't you going just a bit far with the addled Aunt Fiona act?" she countered.

"I haven't told that child a single lie and you know it," Fiona said. "If she had even the vaguest inkling of the real potential of her powers, she'd be so scared she'd run right back to slinging hash in that diner and taking orders from my hare-brained little sister. Is that what you want to have happen, Myrtle?"

"No, of course not," she said, "but Jinx thinks you're giving her the run around, so just try to be a little more forthcoming with your explanations without telling her too much."

"Myrtle, dear," Fiona said sweetly, "you do know the definition of the word 'contradiction?'"

"Well," a new voice said, "this certainly sounds like old times."

Amity Prescott entered the sitting area from her side of the basement. "Hail, hail, the gang's all here," she said, rolling out the wooden desk chair and sitting down. She looked at Myrtle, pointing an index finger toward the ceiling, "They're not going to hear us down here, are they?"

"Sound dampening incantation," Myrtle said absently. "Rodney might hear us, but the girls won't."

"And what about Darby?" Amity asked.

Myrtle gestured over her shoulder. "He's all the way in the back cataloging rare crystals."

"How far is 'all the way in the back?'" Fiona asked.

Myrtle thought for a minute. "I think we put the crystals on Aisle 736."

Amity inclined her head toward the table. "I see Jinx found the quaich," she said.

"Yes," Myrtle replied, "rather easily, in fact. Knasgowa was waiting for her."

"Where was the cup hidden?" Fiona asked.

"In a hollowed out section of the flat boulder across from the waterfall," Myrtle said.

"Nice," Amity said, "Alexander did good work."

"He had a good teacher in Knasgowa," Myrtle observed.

"Can you just imagine?" Amity said admiringly. "Jinx actually spoke with Knasgowa. That's just amazing. That girl is the only one of us, other than you Myrtle, who has ever done that."

"I knew Knasgowa would come to Jinx," Fiona said. "She and Alexander sacrificed everything to bind Brenna to limbo." She looked at Myrtle questioningly. "Did Knasgowa tell Jinx anything else?"

Myrtle nodded. "She told Jinx none of this is her fault."

"And it's not," Chase said, with sudden vehemence. "It's our fault. We should have found a way to give Jinx more guidance while she was learning how to use her powers."

Fiona made a soft, clucking sound in her throat. "Now, now, Chase," she said. "We really didn't think she'd just start Googling spells and trying them out."

"She was trying to *help*," Chase said protectively.

The three women exchanged a knowing look.

"See," Myrtle said, "I told you. He's in love with her."

"Well, now what's wrong with that?" Fiona said brightly. "I think it would be wonderful for one of our clan to be with a McGregor."

"You won't feel that way when the kittens are born," Festus mumbled from the hearth.

"Dad!" Chase said, outraged.

"No werecat has ever produced an offspring with a witch," Festus said, unfazed by his son's reaction. "For all you know, you'll get a human-looking kid with a tail, big ears, and whiskers."

"Stop!" Chase ordered, now blushing outright. "No

one is talking about having kit ... er ... babies. All of you, just *stop*."

Everyone laughed at that, Festus chiming in with a wheezing sound that could have been merriment or an impending hairball. Finally Amity had the good grace to apologize for them all.

"We're sorry, Chase," she said, wiping her eyes. "It's just that we've been trying to fix you up with a girl for years now, and you and Jinx are just so darned cute together."

"We won't be so cute when she finds out what I am," he said. "Seriously, I think the whole shapeshifter thing is just going to be too much for her."

"Right now it probably would be," Amity said, "which is why I agree with you. *That* bit of information can wait until everything else is settled down." She looked over at Myrtle. "Do we have a plan?" she asked. "Those ghosts out there on the square are starting to get rowdy, and that rabble rouser Howard McAlpin isn't helping matters."

Fiona blew out a disgusted blast of air. "That *man!*" she said scornfully. "I thought surely this town was rid of him when someone ran him through with that swordfish trophy."

"He *was* murdered, you know," Myrtle said, as if the news was just a casual aside. "He is right about that."

Amity regarded her with horror. "*Now* you decide to tell us that?" she said. "The whole town buzzed for weeks when he was found with that trophy sticking out of his chest."

"Well, yes," Myrtle replied reasonably, "but not because anyone was actually sorry that he was dead."

"Huh," Amity said, digesting the statement. "I guess that *is* true."

"Who killed him?" Fiona asked eagerly. "Was it a political hit for hire?"

Myrtle laughed. "Hardly anything that exciting," she said. "He cheated in the swordfishing tournament. The rightful winner drove up here from Wilmington to confront him; they argued and the man pushed Howard into the trophy."

"Ah," Fiona said, "that makes perfect sense. Howard couldn't even fish honestly. Don't forget to tell Jinx about the murder at some point. I don't think that insufferable idiot will go quietly back into the grave until he knows the truth about his death."

"I'll put it on the list," Myrtle said, "but there are a few items of greater importance ahead of Howard McAlpin's ego."

"To say the least," Amity agreed. "So, what do you need from all of us tomorrow night when you help Jinx summon Alexander Skea's spirit?"

"At this point, nothing," Myrtle said, "but that may change once we are in possession of the journal."

Chase cleared his throat. "I hate to be the voice of gloom and doom," he said, "but have any of you given any thought to what we're going to do if we *don't* find the journal?"

Myrtle regarded him gravely.

"That," she said, "would be a seriously negative turn of events."

Twenty-Three

Myrtle surprised me with the announcement that we weren't going to immediately use Knasgowa's silver cup to summon Alexander. Was I the only one who wanted this whole mess to just go *away*?

"It will be dawn soon," Myrtle said placidly. "That's not the correct time to be conjuring a spirit. Go upstairs and get some sleep. We'll take this matter up after night-fall."

Sleep was the last thing I wanted to do. I felt absolutely energized. I'd just talked to my own great-great-some-thing-grandmother and had an incredible encounter with a *mountain lion*.

Maybe you'd have to be a cat lover to really understand just how cool that really was. I'm not just crazy about my over-indulged pack of spoiled house cats, I love all cats, and this one had just been . . . *amazing*.

I know, I know. "Amazing" is an incredibly over-used word these days, but I really don't know any other way to describe what it was like staring into those intelligent, amber eyes. It was almost like there was a *person* in there.

Since Tori can fall asleep standing up, she happily dragged off to bed. I curled up on the couch and watched the sun come up, which should have been a cue for the ghosts milling around the courthouse square to disappear.

Except not all of them did.

And somehow, that just made me feel sadder and more determined to undo what I had done. Watching those pale forms wandering aimlessly around the square as the night lightened to day brought the weight of their loneliness home to me.

Unlike Beau and the graveyard regulars who had come to accept their earthbound plight, the spirits I had awakened were confused. They wanted their lives back. The more I watched them, the more convinced I became that I had unwittingly taken them away from something better. Accident or not, I had no right to do that.

That weighed on me, and so did the sensation of basically being a deer caught in the crosshairs of a high-powered scope. Brenna Sinclair was out there somewhere. Since that night when she smiled at me through the darkened store window, I'd looked for some sign of the red-haired sorceress in every shadow.

She hadn't appeared again, but neither had she *disappeared*—at least not from my worried thoughts.

Knasgowa said we might not be able to banish Brenna. *Not* what I wanted to hear, by the way. If we simply took away her mortality, what would Brenna do? What the heck *was* she doing? *Where* was she?

I hated the feeling that we were being watched, which is why I wanted to get on with talking to Alexander Skea. *Now*.

Instead I was made to wait.

I waited while the sun came up.

I waited as I went through the motions of fixing breakfast and feeding the cats.

I waited while I spent the morning restlessly dusting the store Darby had already cleaned to immaculate perfection.

I *waited* fourteen freaking hours until the sun went

down and Myrtle was willing for us to get down to business.

Were my nerves a little on the frayed side?

Uh, *yeah*.

Which is why I plopped down in one of the chairs by the fireplace in the basement, and without bothering about any pleasantries, looked straight at Myrtle and said, "Okay, let's do this thing."

"Impatient, much?" Tori asked, sitting down in the chair next to me.

"I think I need to prepare you for . . ." Myrtle started.

And, of course, I had to go and do something impulsive because I was in such a hurry.

Without waiting for instructions, I picked up the silver cup, cleared my mind, and went for the ride of my life.

Let's just recap my spectral resume up to that moment.

Aunt Fiona was the first ghost I ever saw. She appeared in my kitchen upstairs and talked to me as if it were the most normal thing in the world, all the while using an old piece of string to play with my cats. I didn't realize she seemed so solid because of her proximity to Myrtle.

Then Tori and I went to the graveyard and I met Beau and the others, who weren't solid at all, but were equally benign.

You know about the angry ghost of the murdered girl, but she gets a total pass for her mood.

The one thing that all those ghosts had in common, however, is that they came to me.

The instant I picked up the bowl and let my psychometry kick in, the tables turned.

I went to Alexander.

Or more exactly, I was sucked down a long, dark tube filled with howling cold winds that shot me out into a foggy, steel-blue landscape so surreal it felt like the backdrop for a cubist painting. All the angles were wrong.

There were no buildings or even trees, just a barren desert filled with enormous jagged rocks.

I landed hard, and immediately scrambled to my feet in panic when I realized a dull mumbling surrounded me. Twisting in frantic circles, I searched for the source of the voices that were surely about to trample over me in a chaotic stampede.

Instead, one voice broke through the rumble.

"You are hearing the mortal coil," the man said. "There is no need to fear it."

Whirling around again, I found myself staring at Alexander Skea, but not the version of him I'd seen in the Lodge photo. This man was young and broad chested with powerful arms. He moved toward me with an air of vigor and purpose.

I couldn't help myself. I took a step back.

"The mortal what?" I managed to croak.

"Coil," he repeated with a smile. "It is a poetic term for the troubles of daily life."

He took my hand and bent low to kiss it.

"I've listened to the voices for so long," he said, looking up at me, "I think I would be quite lost without them. I take it my wife sent you?"

Suddenly I remembered why I had come in search of him.

"Yes," I said, "she did, but where are we?"

"We are between your world and the next," he said, "in a nether region that belongs everywhere and nowhere."

Trust me. By this point, I'd completely given up on getting a straight answer from anyone.

Then it hit me. A *nether* region? Wasn't that like another word for limbo?

Choking a little on the words, I asked, "But isn't this where you and Knasgowa sent Brenna?"

His face grew more serious. "No," he said. "We sent

her to a much darker realm, a place where the angels hold back the powers of the night. But she is no longer there, is she?"

The important point for me at the moment was that she wasn't anywhere near where we were standing.

"No," I said. "I'm sorry. That's my fault, but it was an accident. I didn't mean to set her free and I'm really trying to put her back."

Alexander seemed to look at me closely for the first time. "You are afraid," he said simply.

Again with the understatements?

"Yes," I admitted, "very afraid."

He offered me his arm. "Walk with me," he said. "Tell me what has happened."

The courtly gesture reminded me of Beau and I suddenly wished very much that the old soldier were here with me.

Alexander wasn't the source of the creeping unease that nearly immobilized me. The metallic, monochrome landscape pulsated with the constant, low rumbling of an unhappy world. It made my skin crawl.

That sound *alone* was the stuff of nightmares.

Seeing my indecision, Alexander spoke again, "Walking will help," he said. "Motion gives a body purpose."

Purpose.

Okay. Purpose would be good.

I took Alexander's arm and, haltingly at first, then all in a torrent, I told him the whole story as the formless landscape moved past us. When I ended with an account of my conversation with Knasgowa, I said, "She wanted me to tell you that she loves you."

Alexander bowed his head and I saw him swallow hard before he spoke. "And I love her," he said. "If you are her granddaughter by blood, then you are mine as well by the affection I hold in my heart for her. This is what you must do."

Let's just say that's when the bovine by-product hit the rotary device.

When Alexander was done speaking, I gaped at him. "You can't be serious," I finally managed to say.

"I am quite serious," he said. "You must go to my final resting place, open my tomb, and retrieve my journal. Draw Brenna to the site of my wife's grave with the blood of my blood. Hold her fast there within a circle of magic. Speak the words in the journal and consign her once again to the blackness of limbo."

Yeah, that part I got. Or at least most of it.

The bigger problem wasn't something I could explain to Alexander.

He thought he was buried under an ancient oak tree at the edge of a country meadow, which is undoubtedly what the scene looked like in 1864. It was now, as best as I could figure, the parking lot of the local Baptist church.

Ever since this witch thing came up I had been worried about going to hell.

Now it was starting to look like a sure thing.

Alexander got me headed in the right direction to return to my own reality, but it was Tori's insistent voice that led me back up through the tunnel and into the light. When I opened my eyes, I was still holding the cup in my shaking hands. The basement felt ice cold.

"What the *hell* did you think you were doing?" Tori demanded, draping a blanket that had appeared out of nowhere around my shoulders. "I thought we agreed after the whole talking-to-hickory-trees episode that you were going to be careful about what you picked up?"

"Sorry," I said weakly, huddling into the blanket. "I was tired of waiting."

The heavenly aroma of coffee suddenly wafted up around me. I looked down into Darby's worried eyes. "Mistress seems to be cold," he said with concern, holding up a steaming mug of coffee.

I put Alexander's cup down and gratefully accepted the coffee, managing not to splash any of the hot liquid on myself with my shaking hands. "Thank you, Darby," I said. "Your timing is perfect."

The brownie hesitated and then he asked, "Did you see my Master?"

The hopeful note in his voice broke my heart.

"Yes," I said. "Alexander told me everything I need to know."

Still looking uncertain, Darby asked, even more softly, "Is he in an awful place?"

God. What could I say to that?

"It's not the greatest," I admitted, "but he's a strong man. I think the worst part for him is not being with Knasgowa."

Darby nodded his head solemnly. "Theirs is a great love," he said.

Myrtle cleared her throat and I glanced over at her. She didn't look *quite* as disapproving as I expected her to, but almost.

"That was exceedingly imprudent of you," she said through pursed lips. "Please don't do something rash like that again."

Even though I really couldn't make any promises about that, my good Southern girl gene kicked in and I mumbled a contrite, "Yes, ma'am."

I'm really not sure Myrtle believed me, but she apparently decided to let it go. "What did Alexander tell you?" she asked, listening intently as I ran it all down for her.

When I got to the end of the story, I said firmly, "We are going to the church tonight. I cannot stand one more day of this."

To my considerable shock, Myrtle agreed with me, as did Beau Longworth who materialized at the foot of the staircase.

"You must go tonight," he said. "Mayor McAlpin is being rather successful in his organizational efforts. He is now rallying the spirits to stage something called a 'haunt in' of City Hall—during the daylight hours tomorrow. When I left they were singing an old Negro spiritual, 'We Shall Overcome.'"

I frowned. "Singing is bad?" I asked.

"Passersby on the street can hear, but not locate the voices," he said. "A crowd is gathering and they are using their communication devices to take photographs. I do not believe anyone has been successful in capturing an image as of yet, but Mayor McAlpin has vaguely materialized at least twice. Those present are hoping to secure a photograph to do something I believe they referred to as 'going viral?'"

Uh-oh. *Not* good.

Or was it?

"How big is the crowd?" I asked.

"Enough to fill the courthouse lawn," he said, "and more are arriving. I am afraid there are also two paranormal investigation groups in attendance; a woman claiming she can 'channel' the spirits of the dead, and a minister preaching about the end of days. I believe there are also correspondents present."

Tori frowned. "There are people in the crowd writing letters?"

"He means reporters," I said. "How about the local police?"

"There are two law enforcement vehicles parked in front of the courthouse," Beau said. "They seem to be primarily involved in securing the smooth flow of motor vehicles around the square."

Perfect. That meant the entire Briar Hollow Police *and* Sheriff's Department were on the case—and paying absolutely no attention to anything else that was going on in town.

"Beau," I said, "do you think you can help us locate the exact site of Alexander's grave the same way you found the cup?"

"I can try," he said. "In theory the principle is the same."

Tori made a little "ahem" sound. "Uh, excuse me? Voice of reason here." she said.

"What?" I asked.

"How, exactly, are we supposed to dig up part of the Baptist Church parking lot without getting caught?" she said. "Never mind lugging a moldy old skeleton across town?"

"The whole town is paying attention to the square," I said. "If we hurry, we can get in and get out without anyone seeing us. It's *perfect*."

"God," she groaned, "don't say that."

"Why not?"

"Because now something is *guaranteed* to go wrong."

TWENTY-FOUR

The scene on the square was even worse than Beau described. All the parking spots around the courthouse were filled. Some people in pickups were even tailgating. A television crew had set up on the sidewalk in front of George and Irma's grocery store two buildings down. They were talking to Irma under the glare of lights rigged to illuminate the immediate area. I opened my own door just enough to hear what the reporter was saying. Thankfully he was one of those pompous types, so I could hear him over the noise of the crowd.

"Over the past few days in the sleepy community of Briar Hollow, citizens have been plagued by a rash of paranormal events," he said, in a mock dramatic voice. "We are speaking with local businesswoman Irma Reynolds, who captured images of a levitating packaged pastry on her store's security camera. Irma, would you describe this horrifying event for our viewers?"

"Well," Irma said, matching his melodramatic flair perfectly, "first off, it was a Twinkie, which isn't *really* a pastry because it doesn't have a crust, but there is cream filling, so that might count. Anyway . . ."

And there you have it, folks. Investigative journalism at its finest.

Just before I closed the door, I caught sight of Howard

McAlpin standing on the front steps of the courthouse. His face was screwed up in a look of intense concentration that made his cheeks bulge out as if he was trying to blow up a balloon. A crowd of people were standing at the base of the steps holding smartphones at the ready.

I felt Beau float up beside me.

"What the heck is Howie trying to do over there?" I asked the colonel.

"I believe he is trying to make himself visible again," Beau said. "He doesn't have a complete understanding of the process just yet. On his last attempt he was only successful at materializing his left arm."

Just then I heard a woman cry, "Hey! Look! I see a foot."

That touched off a firestorm of camera flashes. From across the lawn, the hellfire and brimstone voice of the self-appointed minister thundered, "It's the devil's claw!"

Well, yeah, but only if Lucifer was buried in his Hush Puppies.

Shaking my head, I closed and locked the door. Tori and I went out the back, using side streets to make a wide circle around to the other side of the square. The Baptist Church was on the edge of town, and the oak tree Alexander Skea described to me sat smack in the middle of the front parking lot.

I parked the Prius behind the Sunday School building and we sat quietly surveying the scene of our impending crime.

"Now what?" Tori asked.

Beau, ever the practical one, said, "I believe I should reconnoiter the location before the two of you expose yourself to view."

I chose not to explore the modern meaning of the phrase "expose yourself" with him.

In less than a second, Beau disappeared from the backseat and reappeared in front of the tree. "Dang," Tori said, "I wish I could do that. It sure would make getting around Walmart during a blow-out sale easier."

"Glad you've got the whole metaphysical realm in proper perspective there, Tori," I said, keeping my eyes on Beau.

"Somebody has to stay realistic around here," she deadpanned.

In spite of the tension I was feeling, I snickered.

"Does this remind you of anything?" she asked.

Of course it did. The first and last time we decided to try cigarettes, for some unknown reason we'd parked behind the church to light up. I think our reasoning was that no one would be there on a Friday night.

"I still say you were blowing smoke in my face on purpose," I said.

"I wasn't blowing it anywhere," Tori said. "I was just trying not to choke to death and catch the fastest case of lung cancer on the planet."

We'd turned to look at one another while we talked, so neither of us caught the fact that Beau had blipped again. His voice from the backseat made us both jump.

"There is an object on the back side of the tree," he said, "but at a rather shallow depth for a grave. I think it's possible the roots of the tree have pushed the body closer toward the surface."

"It's about time we caught a break on something," I said. "Okay, let's go."

Tori and I got out of the car, each extracting a shovel and a pair of work gloves from the backseat.

Beau said, "I suggest you advance across the open ground at the double quick."

"Huh?" Tori said.

"It's military guy speak for run," I explained.

So we did. Scrunching down a little to make our silhouettes less obvious, we made a straight line for the tree. I doubt we looked all paramilitary, but we did at least arrive on the back side of the trunk without tripping and breaking our fool necks. Thankfully, whoever paved the lot left a nice big circle of undisturbed turf and dirt around the tree.

There were no lights on in any of the church buildings and none in the houses across the street, so it was possible we were going to get away with this. While Beau kept watch, Tori and I started to dig. Any of you Baptist Sunday School kids who lost your Hot Wheels in the parking lot? Come by the store. We've got'em.

I don't know how long we worked. The little pile of long lost treasures grew on one side of the growing hole while dirt piled up on the other. It was hard working in and around the roots. Ultimately Beau had to leave his post and bend over us so his glowing form would give us extra light.

Thankfully, neither of us were strangers to working a shovel. As little girls, we'd alternated between playing with dolls and digging in the dirt, which graduated to helping the moms put in their annual gardens. Kelly and Gemma do not think small in this regard. They plant enough to feed a small South American country.

A couple of times we froze when we heard a dog bark or a car pass on the street, but no one turned into the lot or came to investigate. My shirt was damp with sweat by this time and my shoulders were starting to ache. More than once Tori asked Beau if he was absolutely certain there was something buried where we were working, and each time, he said he was.

I think we were about four feet down when the blade of my shovel hit something, making a dull metallic clank that echoed in the night. Without being asked, Beau bent down beside me as I brushed loose dirt away with my gloved hand to reveal the lid of an old-fashioned strong box.

It took another 20 minutes of digging, punctuated with grunts and some words we shouldn't have been using in a church parking lot, but Tori and I finally pulled the box free. Then we just stood there looking at each other.

"Well," she said, giving me the innocent eyes, "open it."

"I don't want to open it," I replied. "There's a dead guy in there. You open it."

Beau cleared his throat. "Given the size of the strong box, there will, at most, be bones inside," he said. "Please forgive my forwardness, ladies, but you really must screw up your courage. You have been quite fortunate to remain undetected up to this point, but I do think you should not . . . what is phrase?"

"Push it," Tori said grimly. "Yeah. Okay. Point taken."

The box wasn't locked, instead the hasp was secured with a metal pin with a clip on one end to hold it in place. Tori took off her gloves and slid the pin free. Then she looked up. "On three?" she asked.

"Yes," I said, putting my own hands on the lid as well. We'd open it together.

"Okay . . . one . . . two . . . three . . ."

As gross as it sounds, whoever put Alexander in that hole waited until there was nothing left of him but bones, which were now neatly stacked inside the box with the skull sitting on top.

Yes, I let out a little girly-girl squeal when I saw the empty eye sockets looking up at me, but Tori said something unladylike so we managed to maintain some game points for bravery.

Right in front of the skull, almost as if Alexander was about to start reading it, a small black leather book rested on what I think were his shin bones.

Without having to discuss what to do next, we closed the lid and Tori slipped the pin back in position. The box was heavy, but we were able to heft it up out of the hole and lug it across the field to where the car was parked. We were going to go back for the shovels and our gloves, but that's when we saw a late model sedan pull into the parking lot.

"Jinksy," Tori hissed, "what are we going to do?"

"Hush," I said. "Let's see what he does."

As soon as the car door opened, I recognized the man; Lamar Weston, the Baptist preacher. He started toward the door of the church with a Bible and a stack of manilla folders under his arm. But then he stopped and peered cautiously toward the oak tree.

He probably saw one of the shovels, but anyway, something caught his attention. He walked over to take a closer look . . . and promptly fell in the hole. Right before he dropped out of sight, we saw his toupee flip up, exposing an expanse of shining bald scalp. Then, a cloud of what I suppose to be sermon notes fluttered up out of the hole.

"That's our cue," I said, starting the car and gliding as quietly as possible onto the street behind the sanctuary. I didn't turn on the headlights until we were two blocks away. Then the giggles hit. We laughed so hard I didn't think I was going to be able to drive. Even Beau was chuckling in the backseat.

Our gasps were punctuated with phrases like "bad rug" and "pit of hell." I don't remember any outright blasphemy, but the irreverence was so thick you could have sliced it with a butter knife.

Tori finally managed to get enough air to say, "We did it, Jinksy."

"Did what?" I asked, wiping mirthful tears from my eyes.

"We finally made the Baptist preacher flip his lid."

That touched off fresh gales of laughter. We were still chuckling when I pulled the Prius into its spot behind the store. Just to be safe, I unlocked the back door and propped it open with a brick before we unlatched the trunk and lugged the strong box inside.

"Hold on a second," I said to Tori. "I want to see what's going on out front."

"That's fine," she said. "I'm going to pop into my place and clean up a little."

Looking down at my own hands, I decided a date with a bar of soap wasn't such a bad idea. I ducked in the downstairs bathroom and turned the water on, feeling guilty about getting the space dirty after all of Darby's hard work.

When I was done, I rinsed off the soap and wiped the sink dry with a paper towel. I pumped out some hand lotion in my palm and walked to the front windows, rubbing my hands together to spread the lotion as I went.

The crowd on the square had thinned a little, but the stalwarts appeared to be in for the long-haul ghost hunt. Some people had even put sleeping bags down in their truck beds, and I spotted a few cameras mounted on tripods. At least the news crew had packed up and moved on to the next breaking story, ratcheting the whole carnival atmosphere down a notch or two.

Howard McAlpin was now sitting on the courthouse steps looking completely exhausted, with the councilmen hovering anxiously around him. I pointed him out to Beau when the old soldier joined me at the window.

"What's up with Howie?" I asked.

"I would imagine he is attempting to regain sufficient energy for his planned protest tomorrow," Beau suggested. "This evening's display must have left him quite depleted."

"I'm sure," I said, "but he's still visible."

"As I warned you," Beau said, "they are all growing

stronger. I fear the good Mayor may actually be able to put on something of a show tomorrow."

"What about the rest of them?" I asked.

The other spirits were wandering aimlessly in the crowd or talking together in little clumps. If I hadn't known that at least 50% of the crowd was dead, the scene looked just like the aftermath of the annual Fourth of July fireworks display

"They are all becoming increasingly frustrated," he said. "Many are fueled by a desperate longing to contact their loved ones. Do you see the lady there, on the bench near the wisteria?"

My gaze followed his pointing finger. The woman sat with her head in her hands, her shoulders heaving with sobs.

"Oh my God," I said, my heart instantly breaking for her. "Why is she crying?"

"She has been trying to speak with her daughter for three days," Beau said. "She fears that because her daughter will not answer, the silence is an indication that the young woman did not love her."

His words made my gut clench, but at the same time, they strengthened my determination.

"Come on," I said, "let's get downstairs."

As soon as Darby saw me and Tori lugging the strong box down the steps, he disappeared into the shelves and came back with a thick blanket that he threw over the work table.

I mean seriously, performing magic with a dead man's bones is no reason to scratch up the furniture, right?

When I withdrew the latch pin and opened the lid, Myrtle peered inside the box, reaching confidently for the leather bound book. She carefully opened the pages, turning them curiously until she stopped at a spot marked by a frayed satin ribbon.

"This is it," she said. "The incantation Knasgowa wrote to imprison Brenna. Now we must find the blood of Alexander's blood."

Remember how I felt about dissection in biology class? Metaphysical chemistry is right up there in the same class of grossness, just dustier.

In an entirely too bright a tone of voice, Myrtle said, "Okay, pick a bone and we'll grind it up."

Affecting a deep bass voice, Tori said, "Fee fi fo fum . . ."

"Don't got there," I warned.

"I smell the blood of an Englishman . . ."

"That's enough, Tori!"

"Be he alive or be he dead . . ."

She was going to do it no matter what I said.

"I'll grind his bones to make my bread."

Great. Now I could never look at flour the same way again.

"Are you happy now, Beanstalk Girl?" I asked.

"Yep," she grinned, "it had to be said."

Giving her a look, I turned back to Myrtle, "I'm not grinding anyone's bones."

The older woman blinked at me a couple of times, obviously puzzled. "But you need to pulverize the bone to work the locator spell."

"Fine," I said, "but I'm not going to be the one to do it."

I swear to you, Myrtle, whom I'm guessing is like a bazillion years old and super powerful herself, rolled her eyes at me.

"As you wish," she said, sounding unbelievably put upon.

We watched as she reached into the box and came up with what I think was a finger bone. Or toe maybe. Anyway, the bone was little. Out of nowhere, Darby appeared with a black cloth and a hammer.

Myrtle spread the cloth on the table, put the tiny bone in the center, folded the material over it, and slammed the hammer down so hard the hinges of the strong box rattled.

"Ewwww," Tori said. "Myrtle! That's disgusting!"

Ignoring the reaction, Myrtle unfolded the cloth and carefully dropped the bone fragments into a mortar, working them with a pestle until she had a fine, white powder.

"There," she said, "that is as much as I can do for you. You have to do the rest."

"The rest of what?" I asked.

Myrtle opened a map of Briar Hollow and spread it out on the table. "We have enough powder to work the spell twice," she said. "I have written the words out."

She reached in the pocket of her sweater and brought out a long, translucent green stone hanging from a silver chain.

"Take a pinch of the powder and dust it over the map," she said. "Hold the amulet perfectly still over the center of the map and read the spell. The amulet will point us to the area where the person with the strongest concentration of Alexander's blood resides. You can then go to that location and work the spell again to find that person."

Even though I wasn't pleased about dipping my fingers in bone dust, I did as I was told. Then I held out the amulet and stared at the words on the little piece of paper. Myrtle had obligingly written them out phonetically.

"Okay," I said, "here goes nothing."

As I started to speak, I felt a frisson of energy move down my arm and into the chain. The amulet began to pulsate faintly, the light slowly intensifying to a steady emerald glow. Then the chain stiffened and moved in jerky circles over the map, right before it lifted out to a 90-degree angle and pointed straight at Tori.

TWENTY-FIVE

One of the things I love about Tori is that she doesn't back up from *anything*. She backed up from this. As she looked down at the green crystal standing taunt at the end of the chain pointing right at her chest, she might as well have been staring down the barrel of a loaded pistol.

No. Wait. I've seen her do that.

When we were both waitresses at Tom's, some drifter off the highway came in and robbed the place. Tori did as she was told and opened the cash register, but she was giving the guy a piece of her mind every second she was doing it, telling him that he was taking money from hard working people.

Afterwards, when she was giving her statement to the local police chief, the cop said, "Tori, for God's sake, you could have gotten yourself killed."

Still fuming, she snapped back, "Well, he made me mad."

So what I was seeing on her face that night was *worse* than the whole loaded gun thing.

Without asking if it was the right thing to do or not, I dropped the amulet and reached for Tori.

I couldn't believe it, but she wouldn't let me touch her.

"Tori," I said, too worried about her to be hurt, "whatever you're thinking right now, just stop. Talk to me."

Her eyes darted to the crumpled chain of the necklace, back up to me, and over to Myrtle. She's the one who saved the day, coming around the table and taking hold of Tori's arms.

"You are not like Brenna Sinclair," Myrtle said simply. "I never would have let you walk in the front door of this shop if you were."

Myrtle has this habit of literally illuminating objects with beams of light, typically in answer to my question about where the heck something is in the store. But she'd done the same thing the night we brought Darby home from the graveyard. Now, as I watched, even though Myrtle was in human form, a warm glow spread out from her and over Tori who immediately relaxed.

She looked at Myrtle uncertainly for a minute and then allowed herself to be engulfed in a motherly hug.

"Are you sure I'm not like her?" Tori mumbled against Myrtle's shoulder.

"Perfectly sure."

I took a step toward them and put my hand on Tori's back. "You okay?" I asked.

She released Myrtle just long enough to throw her arms around me.

"Hey," I whispered against her ear, "you're just exactly who you were five minutes ago. What do I care if some rock shoots you the finger?"

Tori let out a kind of choked giggle. I stood back from her, wiping the tears from her face. "Okay?" I asked again.

She snuffled and nodded. I looked in her eyes and knew she was back with us.

"You know what this means, right?" I asked.

"Not really," she admitted, her voice rough with the tears she was still holding back.

"Slow, much?" I grinned. "It means we're related."

That won me Tori's usual wise-ass grin, which is what

I had been aiming for, but her words weren't sarcastic at all.

"I didn't need some magic Pop Rock to tell me that," Jinksy. "We've been sisters from day one."

Which is true. Our birthdays are three days apart. Our mothers are BFFs. They just plunked us down together on the living room rug and the rest is history. What we'd learned tonight was just confirmation we didn't really need between us. As for the larger ramifications? That I wasn't sure about yet.

I looked at Myrtle. "She has to be descended from Knasgowa, too, right?"

Myrtle nodded. "Yes, but from a child that Knasgowa shared with Alexander Skea."

"Why are we just now hearing about them having a kid?" Tori asked, scrubbing at her face.

Did I mention how much she hates to cry?

Suddenly Darby was by her side holding out a per- fectly ironed linen handkerchief. "Would this help, Miss Tori?" he asked.

For a minute I thought she was going to start blubber- ing again because the little guy can just be so darned sweet. Instead, she accepted the handkerchief, leaned down, and kissed the astonished brownie on the forehead.

"Darby," she said, "you may be nicest man I've ever met."

He didn't need any help from Myrtle to glow at those words.

"Thank you, Miss Tori," he said. "I like you very much, too. And please don't be afraid. If you are a descendant of Master Duncan, he was a good man."

Talk about being slow on the uptake. Of course Darby would have known Alexander's children.

"Okay, let's sit down and talk about this," I said, nudg- ing Tori toward one of the chairs by the fire. She sank down in the leather, still looking a little limp, but her color had come back.

I sat down across from her and looked at Darby who was standing between us. "You said Duncan. Isn't that the name of the man who imprisoned Brenna the first time in the Orkneys?"

Darby nodded. "Yes. Master Alexander named his son after his great-grandfather, Duncan Skea."

"And you knew about this?" I asked Myrtle.

"Yes," she said.

"And you didn't tell us, why?" I didn't even try to disguise the annoyance in my voice.

"Because I was protecting those who carry Brenna's blood," she said. Then, almost apologetically, she added, "I didn't know Tori was one of them."

"How is that even possible?" I demanded. "You're . . . you're . . . well, I don't know what you are, but you're supposed to *know* things."

Myrtle smothered a smile. "The magic in Tori's blood is dormant, just as yours was before Fiona activated it at your request. Because of that Tori didn't attract my attention."

"But you would have known if she was evil?" I asked. "How does that work?"

"Let's just say evil has a different . . . flavor," Myrtle said. "It's really rather complicated and I think we best move on at the moment. I assume you want to know about Alexander and Knasgowa's children."

There was a lot I wanted to know, but she was right.

I nodded and Myrtle started talking. "Alexander and Knasgowa raised their son on the frontier until he was old enough to make his own way in the world. This area was largely unsettled in those days. It was possible for a family to live far removed from the affairs of other men. When Duncan Skea, the younger, left his parents' home and came down out of the mountains, he changed his surname to Scarlett."

Realization dawned on Tori's face.

"Oh my God," she said. "I know that name. The Scarletts are some of Mom's people."

"But you said Knasgowa died here in Briar Hollow," I said. "They never told anyone here that Duncan was their son?"

"No," Myrtle said. "Knasgowa used her magic to cloak her son's identity from Brenna just as she used it to protect Alexander. With the passage of the years, she and Alexander began to feel more secure. They moved into town and were able to enjoy the company of their children and grandchildren in the role of family friends. It was only when Knasgowa grew ill that Brenna was able to find them."

"So Alexander and Knasgowa bound Brenna to protect their family," I said.

"Yes," Myrtle said, "and Tori is descended from those people."

In a quiet voice, Tori asked, "What does that mean? Can Brenna use me to hurt all of you?"

Myrtle shook her head. "No," she said, "not against your will."

"But my whole family has her blood?" Tori said.

"To varying degrees, yes," Myrtle said. "But the amulet chose you because you have the greatest concentration of magic derived from that lineage."

Tori let out a derisive snort. "Come on, Myrtle. Get out of here! I'm not magic."

That's when puzzle pieces started falling into place for me.

"Are you so sure about that?" I asked.

Tori frowned. "Huh?"

"From the start you've been able to see the spirits," I

said. "You've always been able to talk to Myrtle. The first time we discussed Aunt Fiona leaving me her magic, you told me about your mother's people believing all the local lore about witch women. And don't forget, you're the one who saw Aunt Fiona at grandma's funeral."

When I had been reeling from the revelation that my aunt was a witch, Tori told me about watching Aunt Fiona at the service talking to Grandma in the casket. It was a hot day and the roses in the funeral spray were wilted. Fiona spoke a few words and brought the blossoms back to life. She even made some of the little rose buds open up.

Tori's eyes widened. "Oh my God, you're right."

She turned toward Myrtle. "Does this mean I can have powers like Jinksy?"

"We have no way of knowing at this point," Myrtle said, "but with study, you undoubtedly will uncover some degree of abilities. All witches have unique powers."

"Okay," Tori said, "now *that* is cool."

When she said that, *I* finally relaxed.

That statement was *totally* my girl. I thought I'd lost her there for a few minutes.

"There is, however, one thing you are both missing," Myrtle said.

Of course there is.

"What?" I asked.

"The fact that Tori is the blood of Alexander's blood greatly simplifies the matter of consigning Brenna to limbo again and hopefully to returning the wandering spirits to their graves."

Definitely a plus. Kidnapping some local to go perform a ceremony in a graveyard at midnight was not going to put us in the running for Citizen of the Year.

"Well, okay then," Tori said, scooting forward in her chair, "let's do it."

"No," Myrtle said, "I'm afraid it will have to wait until sundown tomorrow. The ritual must be performed at . . ."

"Midnight," Tori and I said in unison.

Did I ever see that one coming?

When Tori and I walked up the basement steps and into the store, I touched her arm. I'm not sure if I didn't want her to be alone or I didn't want to be alone.

"You wanna crash on the couch?" I asked.

She ducked her head a little. "Would I be a big baby if I said yes?" she answered.

"No more than I was when I refused to get in a bathtub for three months after I saw *Jaws* the first time," I teased.

She rolled her eyes. "You're the only person I know who could be worried a great white shark was gonna come up the drain."

"It could happen," I said archly. "Those things are sneaky."

"Hang on a sec while I throw on some pajamas," Tori said, disappearing into her apartment.

When she re-emerged in baggy pajama pants and a worn out t-shirt, we went upstairs together without saying much. From the ghost rave out on the square to parking lot grave robbing and playing metaphysical *Family Feud*, we were both pretty worn out. I helped Tori make up the couch, throwing a blanket over her when she stretched out.

As I turned to head off to bed myself, she caught hold of my hand. The only light in the room came from the front windows, which looked out on the square.

"Love you, Jinksy," she said softly.

I squeezed her hand. "Go to sleep, honey," I said. "I love you, too."

Yeah. Okay. I admit it. I got up about a dozen times to check on her, but unlike me, Tori has the ability to turn her mind off and go to sleep. The cats stayed with her, seeming to understand she needed their company more that night than I did. It was after 3 o'clock before I finally fell asleep.

The last thing I remember thinking before I drifted off was Scarlett O'Hara's famous line from *Gone with the Wind*. "After all, tomorrow is another day." And man, what a day it proved to be.

TWENTY-SIX

Sorry if what I'm about to say takes a little drama out of my story here toward the end, but we *cleaned up* on sales the next day. Howard McAlpin couldn't exactly announce to the world that he intended to stage a "Haunt In" at the courthouse, and he wasn't getting any better at making himself visible. He did, however, excel at agitating all the other spirits. Even when the sun came up, there were just enough unexplained incidents going on to keep the paranormal groupies camped out across the street.

The local law officials probably could have chased them out for loitering or something, but the instant the stores on the square opened, the groupies started spending money. After all, they had to eat, which meant people were lined up outside of George and Irma's door, buying them out of doughnuts and coffee in 30 minutes. Seizing the opportunity, the pizzeria quickly opened up, hanging out a hand-lettered sign offering "Breakfast Pies."

Chase called my cell phone a little after 9 o'clock. "You okay over there?" he asked.

"Yes," I said, "just really busy."

"I won't keep you," he said. "I just wanted to see if you needed anything before I take off."

"Where are you going?" I asked.

"Fishing," he said.

"You *fish*?" I blurted out.

"Flyfishing," he amended. "None of these folks are going to buy anything in a cobbler's shop and the noise is driving me nuts. I'm going to ride my bike up into the mountains and find a nice, peaceful trout stream. I may camp out overnight."

"Have fun," I said, feeling more than a little jealous. "See you when you get back."

By noon, a couple of food trucks arrived, and George and Irma, not to be outdone, were grilling burgers under a makeshift tent on the sidewalk by their front door. Tori and I didn't have much in the way of food to offer, just a few ready-made sandwiches in the refrigerator behind the counter, but those disappeared before 10 A.M.

We did a brisk business in Briar Hollow souvenirs, selling out of t-shirts and sun visors. Since Aunt Fiona's only philosophy in regard to inventory was "more is better," we also unloaded some stray coolers, a few lawn chairs, some picnic blankets, and a couple of canvas tarps which were instantly pressed into service as awnings over pickup beds.

Amity Prescott came in around 2 o'clock to check on us. "Can you believe this nonsense?" she demanded as she strode through the front door.

"Hi, Amity," I said. "How's business at your place?"

"Well," she said, "this isn't exactly the art and regional pottery crowd, but I've had a lot of walk-in traffic for the local craft stuff. All the walking sticks are gone." She looked guilty for a minute and then admitted, "I re-labeled them as wizard's staffs."

I laughed. "Don't feel bad," I assured her. "There's not a single crystal left in the store. Tori hawked every one as a 'protection amulet.'"

"Hey!" Tori protested, coming out of the storeroom at the sound of her name. "It was a matter of striking while the monetary iron was hot."

"So what's the latest sighting over at the courthouse," I asked. We'd already gotten used to the periodic sound of excited shouting from the crowd.

Amity made a grumbling noise in her throat. "I think that latest one was a hovering hand or something. Some woman keeps insisting she hears weeping on one of the benches out on the lawn, and there's a guy who swears he saw a Confederate colonel staring up at the monument."

Uh-oh.

We visited for a few minutes longer and then Amity went back to her place. There were still people in my store, but I really needed to have a word with Beau Longworth.

"You okay to hold down the fort for a few minutes?" I asked Tori.

She had awakened that morning as her usual sunny self. We'd been too busy to really talk, but I didn't sense any of the anxiety or uncertainty I'd felt from her the night before. Tori bounces back like nobody's business.

"I'm good," she said.

"Really?" I asked, looking at her intently.

"Really, Mom," she affirmed. "All these customers are keeping my mind off what we have to do tonight. Go on. Find out what the heck Beau was thinking."

I headed down to the basement, carefully closing the door behind me. Myrtle was nowhere to be seen, but Darby poked his head out from between a row of shelves. "Do you need me, Mistress?" he asked.

"No, Darby, I need to talk to Colonel Longworth," I said. Raising my voice slightly I called out, "Beau? Get down here right now."

After a few seconds, the old soldier appeared in front of me. I didn't even have to tell him what I wanted. When he became visible, he was holding his hands up in front of his body in the classic male pose for, "Honey, I can explain."

"What the heck are you doing showing yourself on the courthouse square in broad daylight?" I demanded.

He gathered himself up. "Unless I am mistaken," he said with exaggerated dignity, "it is to our advantage to have the attention of the crowd and the local constabulary firmly focused on the square until this evening is over; am I correct?"

Well, at least he was up to speed on the plan.

"I'm guessing Myrtle filled you in?" I asked.

"Yes," he said, "when I came last night to give you a report, she told me what happened with Miss Tori. The two of you had already retired for the evening and I thought it best not to disturb you. How is Miss Tori, please?"

His concern was so genuine it took the edge off my annoyance.

"Holding up," I said. "She'll be happier when we get Brenna gone tonight. What were you going to tell me last night?"

Beau let out a frustrated sigh. "That Mayor McAlpin is quite hopeless," he said. "I do not believe I have ever encountered anyone with less talent for being deceased. The man could not solidify his whole form to save his life."

I decided to ignore that oxymoron.

"So he's still just flashing body parts every few minutes?" I asked.

"Yes," Beau said, shaking his head. "He seems to have gained a measure of control over materializing his left hand, so he is engaging in a great deal of finger pointing."

No doubt a skill the man also possessed when he was breathing.

"So that's what people are shouting about over there?" I asked. "A floating hand?"

"For the most part," Beau said, "but even though the woman on the bench continues to wail inconsolably, I became concerned that the interest of the crowd was waning. In appearing at the base of the monument, I was merely attempting to give them something slightly more . . . coherent . . . on which to focus."

Oh my God. The man was a genius.

"Can you get the other cemetery regulars to help with that?" I asked. "Can any of them appear in daylight?"

Beau knew instantly what I had in mind.

"A few of them, yes," he said, "and there does seem to be a sort of amplification of available energy for us at the moment."

"Perfect," I said, "get them into town. Have Jeff throw a few forward passes over the lawn, and oh, can you bring Duke, too? That crowd will love a ghostly coonhound."

"I can," he said. "Duke is a most intelligent canine specimen. He will be overjoyed to be taken on an outing."

"Okay," I said, "don't go crazy or anything, just keep everyone's attention on the square."

He started to fade out, but I stopped him. "What the heck is Howie trying to do with all that pointing?" I asked.

Beau's form solidified. "He continues to espouse a great deal of nonsense about spectral civil rights," Beau said, "and he is now on a tirade regarding corruption in local politics. He is literally pointing out offenders and reciting their infractions."

Huh. Never pass up the chance to build up a little reserve of dirt.

"Can you kinda take notes on what he's saying?" I asked, looking a little guilty about the request.

I shouldn't have worried. Beau flashed me a dashing grin. "A good soldier never ignores potentially useful intelligence." With that, he touched the brim of his hat and was gone.

Beau and his crew did an outstanding job for the rest of the day. By sundown, the crowd around the courthouse was back up to full strength. George and Irma were flipping burgers like pros, and I can't even imagine how many tons of pizza were being sold over at the Stone Hearth.

The news crew was back, and there were even more vans scattered around the square bearing the logos of paranormal investigative groups. I finally shoved the last customers out the door around 7 o'clock, flipping the "Open" sign over to "Closed" and vehemently shaking my head at a small knot of people begging me to relent.

Turning off the last of the store lights, I descended to the basement where Darby had laid out supper for us. The minute the heavenly scent of pot roast hit my nostrils, I realized I was starving.

As I joined Tori at the table, I was pleased to see she was eating heartily. It was one thing to see my BFF scared, but if she pushed back the supper plate, we were *really* in trouble.

Myrtle was sitting at the table, too, but she wasn't eating. I wasn't even sure she *needed* to eat.

"So, what's the plan?" I asked, reaching for the mashed potatoes.

While we'd been shamelessly making money off of this whole mess, Myrtle had been studying Alexander Skea's journal.

"I have devised a potion that will make Tori something of a . . . beacon," Myrtle explained. "As soon as she drinks it, her blood will call out to Brenna."

"How do you know Brenna will answer?" I asked.

"She will answer," Myrtle said gravely. "Hers is an old and fervid ambition."

"And we'll be ready for her?" Tori asked, buttering a biscuit.

"Yes," Myrtle said. "Before you use the potion, Jinx will follow my instructions to create a magic circle around

Knasgowa's grave. When Brenna comes to you, she must be standing inside the circle when you close it."

"How do we do that?" Tori asked, chewing.

The answer made her choke on her biscuit. I had to lean over and thwack her on the back several times until she could breathe again.

"I have to do what???" she finally managed to ask.

With forced patience, Myrtle repeated herself. "You will slice the palm of your hand with a ritual dagger and drip the blood onto the earth. The magic in your blood will seal the three of you inside the circle, and render Brenna temporarily powerless. Jinx will recite the spell, and Brenna will be bound."

Uh-huh. That sounded just a little too easy. Well, okay, not the slicing part but the rest of it. When I pointed that out, Myrtle said, "Well, to steal a line from Dylan Thomas, she may not go gently into that good night."

Yeah. I passed high school English.

"Isn't there another line in that poem that goes, 'Rage, rage against the dying of the light?'"

Myrtle sighed, "Once the circle is closed, Brenna will be deprived of her magic only. She will, undoubtedly, attempt to fight you. If you cannot hold her back and she succeeds in pushing Tori over the boundary of the circle, its protection will be shattered and you will be facing Brenna and her powers at their full strength.

Fantastic. We were about to play a circular version of Red Rover with a chick who was undoubtedly a big ole cheater.

"And if that happens?" I asked.

"Then I am afraid you will have to . . . improvise," Myrtle said.

This was just getting better and better.

"Fear not," Colonel Longworth said, materializing on the stairs and walking toward us, "you will not be alone."

Uh, yeah, we would.

"No, Beau," I said, holding up my hand when he started to protest, "no arguments. You're staying in town. What could you do against Brenna anyway?"

"Wel, I . . . I . . ." he spluttered indignantly.

"Exactly," I said.

To my horror, the old gentleman actually looked hurt.

I shoved my chair away from the table and went to him, grateful that I could actually touch him in Myrtle's presence.

"Beau," I said softly, "you are the bravest man I know. Thank you for wanting to be there to protect us, but I need you to handle the rear guard action."

Yep, that was me being all military. I'd been studying the lingo. When you talk to a Civil War soldier as much as I do, it's necessary.

"But Miss Jinx," he said reproachfully, "I have always ridden *toward* the sound of the guns."

Of that, I had no doubt. Something told me Beauregard T. Longworth never backed down from a fight in his whole life, and he wasn't about to start sounding retreat after his death either.

"I know that, Beau," I said, intuitively understanding part of what was bothering him. "This is not like what happened to your men. Tori and I will be fine. You did not let your boys down, and you won't be letting me down if you stay in town tonight. This is where I need you to be."

That wasn't quite the truth. I didn't want my ghostly friend anywhere near magic designed to consign a spirit to limbo.

Beau looked at me for a long moment. "You are so like my daughter," he said finally. "I cannot bear it if you are harmed, Miss Jinx."

Tears filled my eyes. "It's okay, Beau," I said. "You can help me more by staying here and keeping everyone's attention off that graveyard. Please?"

He nodded. He wasn't happy about it, but he would do as I asked.

I turned back to Myrtle. "Okay, so I get the plan with Brenna, but what about the spirits I raised? What will happen to them?"

"I believe they will be returned to their graves when you recite Alexander's spell," Myrtle said.

"You believe?"

She took off her glasses and rubbed her eyes. "Truthfully, Jinx, I'm not sure how you raised them in the first place, but restoring the pre-existing state of Knasgowa's grave is our best chance of fixing that situation as well. That is, as you say, all I've got."

Well, okay, at least she was honest about it.

I looked at Tori. "You good with this plan?"

"Yes," she said, "but do we have time for pie, first?"

TWENTY-SEVEN

We were used to the cemetery bustling with otherworldly activity at night. Now it was dark, deserted, and decidedly spooky—which I guess anyone else would have called "normal" for a graveyard.

Tori and I were working at Knasgowa's grave. Myrtle had explained to us both how to draw a circle around the plot with a simple stick. I had been hoping for a magic wand, but apparently the magic is always in the practitioner, not in the props.

Once the circle was complete, I used the stick to carefully trace off a series of symbols at the four points of the compass. Tori followed along behind using the LED on her cellphone to check my work for accuracy.

At the stroke of midnight, I held a small glass bottle with a cork stopper out to her. "Okay," I said, "here you go. Bottoms up."

She took the bottle and met my eyes. "Remember what you said to me that night at the tree?"

"I asked you to pull me out of there if I got in trouble."

"Same deal?" Tori asked.

"Same deal," I said. "I'll be right here with you."

Working the cork out of the bottle, she sniffed the liquid and made a face. "Dear God," she said, "I hope it tastes better than it smells."

"Don't count on it," I warned. "Take it like a tequila shot."

Uh, yeah. We've chased the worm a few times.

In one smooth motion, Tori upended the bottle and gulped down the dark liquid. Even taking the potion at top speed, she started to cough violently.

"Don't spit," I ordered. "Myrtle said take it all."

Tori nodded, her face screwed up in revulsion.

"Bad?" I asked.

"You have no idea," she croaked.

"How do you feel?"

She looked at me like I'd lost my mind. "Like I'm gonna hurl," she said.

"Yeah, I got that part. What else?"

She considered the question. "Kind of hot," she said, "you know, like how the moms bitch about their hot flashes?"

"Is that all?"

Tori shook her head. "Pretty much," she said. "Do you think maybe it didn't work?"

A sultry voice spoke in the night.

"I assure you, it worked."

We both jumped. Brenna Sinclair stepped out of the darkness. She was still dressed all in black and her dark red hair flowed down over her shoulders, but the dramatic cloak was gone. I blinked and looked closer. She was wearing black jeans, high-heeled black boots, and a matching silk tunic.

"Well," I said, "look at you going all fashion modern. Can't say much for your color sense though. Have you had your chart done?"

The talk was tough, but I was shaking like a leaf.

Brenna gave me a slightly more feral version of the smile I'd seen that first night through the store window. "Bravado becomes you, little witch," she said.

Then she turned the weight of those green eyes on Tori, sending her gaze traveling over my friend with a kind of lurid interest that made my blood run cold. "Hello, grand-daughter," Brenna said.

"Bite me," Tori snapped.

Brenna threw her head back and laughed. The sound of her voice was like a living thing, dancing around us with such presence I resisted the urge to take a step back.

"Oh," she crooned, "I do so enjoy it when you pathetic little creatures posture. When I show you what the force of real magic is like, Victoria, you will become as magnificent as I am."

No self-esteem issues there.

"You want me, lady?" Tori asked. "Then come get me."

Brenna's green eyes glittered. "Don't you think I know what you're doing? You want me to step across your adorable little circle. Fine, I'll come to you, but you'll never be strong enough to hold me."

She couldn't have been more than a dozen steps away from us, but in the length of time it took her to cross that distance, I knew exactly how a mouse feels staring up into the jaws of a cat.

Even if she hadn't been a sorceress, Brenna was formidable. Her tall, lean body moved with a contained energy that was seductive and repellent all at the same time. She stopped just outside the boundary of the circle.

"Ready to play with Mommy?" she purred.

"Bring it," Tori said, through clenched teeth.

As Brenna stepped over the line, Tori pulled out the dagger Myrtle had given her and used it to gash her palm. The instant the blood drops hit the ground, we were encased behind walls of prickling energy.

Brenna lunged for Tori, and to my surprise, Tori raised the knife and drove it in the woman's shoulder.

"Jinx," Tori yelled, "get busy!"

I started chanting the words Myrtle forced me to memorize as Brenna pulled the dagger out of her shoulder and wiped the blade on the sleeve of her silk blouse.

"That wasn't very nice," she said in a reproving singsong voice. "I'm afraid you're going to have to pay for that."

But instead of attacking Tori, Brenna swept the knife toward me.

I wasn't ready, but I managed to get my arm up and deflect the blade anyway. I knew she'd cut me because I felt the warm trickle inside my sleeve, but I'd bought enough time to back away—or so I thought. No sooner did I start to move than I tripped on a root and fell.

Truthfully? The biggest advantage I have in life is dumb luck.

The cut on my arm was deeper than I realized. When I landed, my blood splattered the ground over Knasgowa's grave mixing with Tori's blood.

Bolts of blue lightning shot through the circle, the same blue lightning I'd once used to drive back an angry spirit.

A look of horror came over Brenna's face. "What have you done?" she cried.

As we watched, the lightning bent and strained, wrapping around Brenna until it formed a pulsating coil. Although she struggled against the electric restraint, Brenna Sinclair could not move.

Tori edged around the struggling woman and helped me up. "How bad are you hurt?" she asked.

"Don't worry about that," I said. "I know what we have to do. Put your hand over the cut on my arm."

"What?!"

"Just do it, Tori," I insisted.

"But, I don't understand . . ."

"The blood," I said fiercely. "Our blood."

Comprehension filled her gaze. She clamped her hand

over my arm. The magic in our bloodstreams fused and her eyes began to glow the same blue as the lightning. I saw my own eyes reflected in hers and we turned as one toward Brenna.

"Oh, Mommie Dearest?" Tori called out. She waited until Brenna's head snapped toward us to finish. "Time for you to go to hell," she said.

A roaring sound rose around us, the blue light building to blinding intensity, and then we were standing there alone in the cemetery, caught in the last swirling breaths of a dying wind. Tori was still holding my arm and I sagged against her a little as a wave of dizziness overtook me.

"Jinksy!" she cried, snaking her arm around my waist to hold me up. "Stay with me."

I shook my head to clear it as Tori led me over to a stone bench. Sinking down gratefully, I watched as she peeled off her over shirt and used it to wrap my arm. "We need to get you to the emergency room," she said.

When I didn't answer her, she raised her voice, "Hey, you're not going into shock on me, are you?"

"No," I finally answered, "look."

The spirits came from all directions. They were so peaceful, they almost looked like they were sleepwalkers heading back to their warm beds, which is really more or less what they did. One by one they found their graves, stretched out, and simply melted back into the earth. It took almost an hour.

The weeping woman from the courthouse bench was one of the last ghosts to return. She paused for just a moment in front of us and studied my face. "Thank you," she said.

"Your daughter couldn't hear you," I said. "It's not that she didn't love you."

"I know," the woman said with a smile. "I didn't before, but I do now. Good night."

"Good night," I whispered as she glided past and slipped back into her grave.

That's when I saw the mountain lion again, sitting at the edge of the graveyard just watching us. Just as they had done the night before, his amber eyes met mine. As crazy as this sounds, I felt like he was telling me I'd done a good job. After a few seconds, the big cat stood up, turned, and padded away.

Tori drew the shirt back to check my cut and gasped.

"What?" I asked.

She pulled the fabric back and I saw that my arm was completely healed. There was nothing left from the wound but a pale, fine scar.

"Let me see your hand," I said.

Tori turned her palm up. Her cut was healed as well. She sat down beside me on the bench. "Did all of that just happen?" she asked.

"I think so," I said.

"Is Brenna gone?"

"I really don't know," I admitted, "but at least the spirits are back where they belong."

"What about the others?" she asked anxiously. "Our friends?"

"There's only one way to find out," I said. Screwing up my courage, I called out, "Beau?"

To my immense relief, the Colonel materialized in front of me. "Are you both unharmed?" he asked anxiously.

"We're fine," I said. "What happened in town?"

"The spirits all looked up at the same time as if someone had called to them," he said. "They began streaming away from the square. I assume they came here?"

"Yes," I said. "They all returned to their graves, and you're still here."

He looked down at me and smiled. "I am where I wish to be."

"And the rest of the regulars?"

Before he could answer, I heard a happy yelp and watched as Duke, the ghostly coonhound, came galloping into the graveyard. He dropped a glowing tennis ball at Beau's feet, looking up at him expectantly.

As the old soldier bent to pick up the ball and throw it, he said, "I would say all is back as it should be."

Twenty-Eight

It's tempting to say everything went back to normal, but there's a lot of truth to the saying that "normal" is just a setting on the dryer. So much has changed—yet again—in such a short time that Tori and I both have some adjusting to do.

For starters, what we did in the cemetery when we fused our blood only seems to have strengthened the bond between us. I won't say that we can exactly read each other's minds, but we've come close a couple of times. Myrtle says that may be the beginnings of a telepathic connection or it could be temporary. She isn't sure.

We haven't heard anything else from Brenna Sinclair and I can't see Knasgowa again until the moon is full, so we're just hoping for the best on that one. Alexander Skea's bones are safe in the basement along with the silver cup. We had a kind of second funeral for him, putting the strong box in a crypt set in the wall. Darby keeps fresh flowers in a sconce nearby.

As for the little guy, he and Tori are deep in plans for the coffee house. All the renovations are finished, the equipment is installed, and we're set to have a grand opening party in about a week. Amity and Chase are keeping their shops open the night of the party. We're hoping to host these events on a regular basis.

One thing we didn't anticipate was that Howard McAlpin flat refused to go back into his grave. He is now the courthouse ghost in residence, but I have to tell you, he sucks at the job. The guy still can't materialize anything but single body parts, but at least he's quit calling for his death to be avenged since the truth about his crooked fishing victory is out.

Things at the cemetery are business as usual with one major change; the ghosts are free to come and go as they please. Most of them choose to stay where they are, but Beau is a regular in the shop and on the courthouse square. He now regards himself as a vital part of the Briar Hollow economy.

You see, the episode on the square put the town on the paranormal map, but as ghosts go, Howie is pretty lame. About once a week or so, when he knows he has a decent audience, Beau appears on the courthouse square. I mean seriously, a Confederate colonel in full uniform at the base of a memorial? The staging couldn't be more perfect.

The tourists are eating it up and all the businesses on the square are thriving as a result. There's even talk that some of the empty buildings are going to filled soon with new shops.

So all in all, I guess the whole mess came out the best way it could. Of course Tori and I have roughly a million questions about our heritage, which means we're going to have to suck it up and talk genealogy with the moms. Myrtle knows a lot, but we need names and dates to fill it all in.

Tori is studying with Myrtle now, too, and my BFF is beginning to feel the first stirrings of her own power. She's getting to take the magic at her own pace, and I'm happy for her. Just having it dumped in your lap can be tough.

You're not going to believe this, but Aunt Fiona actually sent me a postcard. From Rio of all places. It seems she's interested in a guy named "Ramone." I chose not to mention that to Beau. I have no idea why Fiona decided to communicate through something as mundanely mortal as the post office, but her penmanship is fantastic.

As for me, I've learned my lesson. No more spells off the Internet. I've also decided that I need to be who I am. If Chase and Amity and I are going to be more or less working together—and if Chase and I are going to have a future—I have to tell them the truth about myself. I don't quite know how I'm going to do that yet, but it's on the short list.

Right now? All I really want to do is enjoy the rest of the summer in peace and quiet.

That's not too much to ask, is it?

EPILOGUE

Betty Montague watched her out-of-town client slowly circle the empty building. The woman had walked into the real estate office that morning inquiring about commercial buildings for sale on the square. Betty had been lucky enough to be first in line for cold calls.

In a slightly foreign accent, the woman described her plans to open a "culinary shop and bakery." Was a suitable building available? Was there ever! The old corner cafe was the perfect spot and the one piece of property her office hadn't been able to move for five years—but, of course, Betty didn't say that. If she managed to close this deal, she'd pick up her usual commission *and* a bonus for moving the office white elephant.

After Betty ran down all the features of the building, talked about the low local taxes, the seasonal tourist trade, and the wonderful "local ambience," the client asked for a few minutes to just "feel the space."

Now, as Betty watched, the woman moved to the large front window and stared at the row of stores directly across from the courthouse. Trying to read her mind, Betty said, "I don't think you need to worry about George and Irma giving you much competition. They're just running an old-fashioned little corner grocery store over there."

"How lovely," the woman muttered, still staring out the window.

"Right next door to them is Aggie's dress shop," she said, "and then you've got Amity Prescott's art gallery, and Jinx Hamilton's place. Jinx sells a little bit of everything, and they have just put in a coffee bar, but they're doing real fancy stuff. If you just make regular coffee, I know folks will want it with their pastries."

Betty knew she was trying too hard, but she couldn't help babbling when she was nervous. In her mind she was already running through all the bills she could pay off with that bonus money.

"Then on the other side of Jinx there's a cobbler shop," she added. "They'll all be great neighbors. And on the street over . . ."

"Who runs the cobbler shop?" the woman asked.

"Oh," Betty said, "a real nice young man named Chase McGregor."

"McGregor? Is that a Scottish name?"

"Don't all names from Scotland start with 'Mc'?" Betty asked, sounding perplexed.

The woman turned to face her, the light from the window throwing an odd halo around her deep red hair. "Not all of them," the woman said. "I am of Scottish descent."

"Really?" Betty said. "I thought Sinclair was an English name."

"No," the woman said, "it's Scottish, and I will take the building. Can you get the papers drawn up today?"

Betty was so excited she could barely manage to answer. "Yes," she stammered, "of course."

"And I assume cash is an acceptable means of payment?"

"You mean cash as in cash money?" Betty asked, her eyes going wide.

The woman smiled tolerantly, "Yes, cash money."

"Cash is good," Betty said, her head bobbing up and down. "Cash is fine. Let me just call the office and tell them to get started on the contract." She paused with the phone in her hand. "I'm sorry, this is so embarrassing, but did you say your first name is Brenda?"

The redhead fixed her with a dazzling smile. "No," she said. "There is no 'd.' My name is Brenna, Brenna Sinclair."

About the Author

Juliette Harper is the pen name used by the writing team of Patricia Pauletti and Rana K. Williamson. As a writer, Juliette's goal is to create strong female characters facing interesting, challenging, painful, and at times comical situations. Refusing to be bound by genre, her primary interest lies in telling good stories.

Six of Juliette's series are currently available. The best-selling *Lockwood Legacy*, is a nine-book chronicle of the lives of three sisters who inherit a ranch in Central Texas following their father's suicide. The first six novels appeared in 2015: *Langston's Daughters, Baxter's Draw, Alice's Portrait, Mandy's Father, Irene's Gift,* and *Jenny's Choice.* The seventh, *Kate's Journey*, will be available early in 2016.

Descendants of the Rose is the first installment of the Selby Jensen Paranormal Mysteries. The second book, *Lost in Room 636*, will also be available in 2016. Selby's business card reads "Private Investigator," but to say the least, that downplays her real occupation where business as usual is anything but normal.

And don't miss the hilariously funny "cozy" *Study Club Mysteries*, a light-hearted spin off of *The Lockwood Legacy*. Set in the 1960s, this series takes on the often-absurd eccentricities of small town life with good-natured, droll humor. The first book, *You Can't Get Blood Out of Shag Carpet*, is already listed in the Amazon store with *You Can't Put a Corpse in a Parade* coming soon.

Juliette has also made forays into the arena of short fiction arena with *Before Marriage*, a light, sweet romance and *Langston's Ghost*, a short-story companion to *The Lockwood Legacy* books.

Fermata: The Winter is the first in a four-novella post-apocalyptic survival series. Five years after an unknown virus divided the world into the living and the dead, four survivors stumble into a winter sanctuary. Brought together by circumstance, but bound by the will to stay alive, a concert pianist and a girl from South Boston forge a friendship and a purpose to cope with their new reality.

Juliette's newest series, *The Jinx Hamilton Mysteries* opens with *Witch at Heart*, a lighter paranormal tale featuring a heroine who possesses powers she never dreamed existed. Jinx has been minding her own business working as a waitress at Tom's Cafe and keeping up with her four cats. Then she inherits her Aunt Fiona's store in neighboring Briar Hollow, North Carolina *and* learns that her aunt has willed her special "powers" to Jinx as well. They say admitting you have a problem is the first step and Jinx has a major problem. She's a new witch and she has no earthly clue what that means—until she's given the opportunity to use her magic to do a good thing.

In Book 2, *Witch at Odds*, Jinx accepts her new life as a witch and is determined to make a success of both that and her new business. However, she has a great deal to learn. As the story unfolds, Jinx sets out to both study her craft and to get a real direction for her aunt's haphazard approach to inventory. Although Jinx can call on Aunt Fiona's ghost for help, the old lady is far too busy living a jet set afterlife to be worried about her niece's learning curve. That sets Jinx up to make a major mistake *and* to figure out how to set things right again.

*Want to know more about
author Juliette Harper?*

*Visit Juliette Harper's home on the web at
http://www.julietteharper.com*

14734261R00141

Printed in Poland
by Amazon Fulfillment
Poland Sp. z o.o., Wrocław